TELL TALES VOLUME II
THE SHORT STORY ANTHOLOGY

EDITED BY RAJEEV BALASUBRAMANYAM
with COURTTIA NEWLAND

TELL TALES

in association with
flipped eye publishing

A Tell Tales Paperback
Tell Tales, London

Published in association with flipped eye publishing limited
P.O. Box 43771, London, W14 8ZY

First Published in the United Kingdom 2005.

ISBN: 1-905233-02-7

The publication of this book was made possible thanks to a grant from
Arts Council England
Printed in the United Kingdom

Acknowledgements

Tell Tales is grateful to Arts Council England for its financial assistance. We would also like to thank; Shilland for PR support, the Bloomsbury Theatre for their willing partnership, the BBC Roots initiative, the readers who helped make Tell Tales Volume I such a successful anthology, and all our regional partners. Most importantly, we would like to thank all the writers who have contributed to Tell Tales over the years, who, in spite of the focus required to carve out successful careers of their own, always find time to contribute to the Tell Tales family.

Courttia Newland
Marrianne San Miguel
Nii Ayikwei Parkes
May 2005

CONTENTS

Foreword

I was trying to list to stories I cannot forget, the ones I don't need to read because they're already a part of me. I came up with four. *The Ramayana, The Mahabharata, Robin Hood,* and *The Three Musketeers.*

Why these?

Because these were the ones my father told me when I was a child.

As we grow older we are taught not to value stories unless they are seen to be serious, seen to be 'literature'. And yet, the best part of our psyches are built from stories. They explain things we can't put into rational terms; they put us in contact with each other in ways where ordinary communication fails. It seems that, in becoming so preoccupied with what is or isn't literature, and what is and isn't 'good literature', we have lost touch with the power of storytelling that existed before critical theory and book reviews. Today, when I read novels, I can divide them into two camps: those that I'm reading, and those that, while reading them, feel like I'm being *told* a story.

In remembering those stories my father told me, or rather, in not remembering, because they live in that part of my mind that doesn't distinguish between today and ten years ago, I learned the following – a story doesn't exist until it is read, but a story doesn't truly breathe until it is told.

Here we have twenty tales, all by accomplished writers, all original, and all possessing that potential to enter the soul and never leave. Read them in your head, read them out loud, read them to others, *tell* them to others, and I hope they will do you for what the stories my father told me did for me.

Rajeev Balasubramanyam, 2005

vii

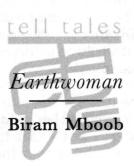

tell tales

Earthwoman

Biram Mboob

The sun was rising, splaying the room with purple veins. Having long ago dispensed with the need for sleep, Shayla had sat through the night examining her latest treasure. It was a leather bound object that one of her husbands had found on a foray into the mountains. She was sure that it was a look-see of some sort. As with all the other look-sees, it was adorned with strange markings she could not understand. Still, she had toyed with it all night, examining each brittle page as if she could decipher the markings through sheer determination.

The quiet was broken by a clatter of morning noises. Her husbands were waking up. Shayla had twelve husbands; any more than that number was forbidden. Twelve was sacred, the uppermost boundary of all things. The Earth breathed in twelves.

Her husbands would soon be busy tending to the squawking children, making the morning meals, breaking wood and fetching water. They worked well together, rarely needing to be chastised or beaten. After the morning routine they would go to the ranch for much of the day. This was mostly just to keep them out of trouble; their agricultural skills left much to be desired when they were unsupervised.

She thumbed through the look-see absently, her concentration broken by the bustle of the morning. She wondered again whether she should show the look-see to her Matriarch. It would be indiscreet, but it would at least satisfy her curiosity.

There was a knock at her door.

She slipped the look-see beneath her robes as her daughter, Lalya, entered. All her children were precious to her as she had only a few that the Sun's rays had permitted to survive. Still, among them all, Lalya was her most favoured, her most promising. Her daughter stood, staring at her, waiting for some sign, some inferred permission to proceed. Shayla ignored her for a little while, testing whether her daughter's patience was maturing as it should be. After a few minutes, Shayla nodded ever so slightly.

'Is Ateph going to die?' Lalya asked.

Shayla frowned. Ateph was her oldest husband and Lalya's father.

'He might do,' she answered. 'Why do you ask?'

'Ateph said he is sick and is going to die soon, but I will live forever and I must try to remember him.'

Shayla winced and made a note to chastise her husband. Even if he was on his deathbed, he had no business meddling in women's affairs, much less confusing a child. She took her daughter in her lap.

'Everyone dies my dear. Ateph is dying sooner because he is sick.'

From mother to daughter, gentle lies.

10

Her words were well measured, well paced, well practised. Her daughter would one day need to fully understand the balance of nature, but for now she was too young. Lalya's father was dying, not because he was sick as he had claimed, but because he was old – and because he was a man. As they were women, old age would never come to her or her daughter. This was the balance of nature. Not even the highest of the Matriarchs truly understood why it was so. As always, tales and legends had sprung to fill the void of understanding. One myth had it that the masculine was still repaying a sin committed in ancient times, born with a hereditary stain that followed them through the ages and cursed them with short, brutish lives. With life spans of only seventy years or less, there was simply not enough time for the masculine to mature, let alone come to understand the true nature of reality. A girl, on the other hand, could not even be considered grown-up until she was at least two hundred.

But not even the Matriarchs, who had lived countless millennia, would think of themselves as immortal. It was not possible for a woman to die of old age, but death could still come in many guises. A rockslide or a sunstorm could end a life in an instant, regardless of its vintage. As such, immortality was an unlikely proposition. Shayla herself was more than six hundred years old. In her life she had buried more husbands and sons than she cared to count. After so long she was nearing her time of *Majj*, sexual maturity, and would soon be able to reproduce by force of will alone. But even after *Majj* she would have husbands. If all Matriarchs in the Rift Valley stopped taking husbands once they reached maturity then the men would starve. There were too few peoples in the Rift as it was and each life was held precious.

She looked at Lalya, the life that she now held most precious in her own heart. Many years from now, Layla would want to know why her brothers were withering away while she and her sisters lived on as centuries passed. For now though, simple answers would do.

'Go tend to your father,' she said, with a note of finality. Lalya obeyed without question, much to Shayla's approval.

Shayla stayed in her room and watched from the window as her husbands left for the ranch, troupes of children in tow. Like all women, Shayla was tall and handsome. Her husbands were short and squat, with small, intensely complicated faces. They were morose and boisterous at turns, childlike in their manners, but equally childlike in their devotion to her. She counted eleven of them, for a brief moment almost forgetting that Ateph was on his deathbed. Poor Ateph. She had intended to go and see him, perhaps even chastise him for his earlier foolishness, but now her every thought was bent on the look-see that nestled in her robes. It occurred to her that she would have no rest until she had learned what stories such a large, ornately bound thing held within it. She made the decision to take it to her Matriarch.

She checked that the homestead was empty then began the short walk through the hamlet. There were many small towns and settlements in the Rift Valley, all of them similar in many ways. Scattered clumps of *enkang* buildings fashioned out of shiny alabaster stone, all loosely arranged near a source of water; in the case of Shayla's hamlet, a clear blue stream that trickled relentlessly from the mountains. There were other women about, and a few errant husbands who were obviously malingering from their daily ranch work. She met the former with greetings and the latter with light reprimands.

After passing many dwellings she came to the place of her Matriarch, the woman that had given her life six hundred years ago. Her Matriarch was standing outside, looking into the purple sky. As Shayla approached she pointed at the sun.

'She is angry today,' her Matriarch said gravely.

The Sun was always angry, her surface always bubbling with dark boils that would burst every so often in flashes of purple. The old myths claimed that She had once been bright white, but Shayla could not imagine such a thing. The story went that the old people had fashioned a giant metal bird with wings of shiny glass and sent it to Her in homage. She had accepted the gift with much joy. But the old people were crafty – they had really sent the bird to steal Her power for themselves. On discovering their treachery, She had turned purple in Her choking rage and had scoured the Earth with flame. Time passed beyond measure, yet still Her fury remained unquenched. The story of course was only a myth; an old husband's tale fashioned to scare children, but She would sometimes still rain licks of fire onto the Earth as if to remind all living creatures that Her power was Hers alone.

'Do you think She will rain today?' she asked her Matriarch.

'She is angry today,' her Matriarch repeated. 'I will send for my husbands before sundown. You should do the same.' She then took her eyes off the Sun and looked at her daughter pointedly.

'What is that beneath your robes?' she asked sharply.

Shayla flinched. After six hundred years she was still unused to her Matriarch's skill at detecting a daughter's subterfuge.

'It is a look-see. I wanted to show it to you,' Shayla

13

said cautiously.

Her Matriarch raised a curious brow and went inside. Shayla followed. They sat at her alabaster stone table in silence for a few moments.

'There is nothing in look-sees of value to you,' her Matriarch stated, folding her arms.

Shayla had already prepared her answer.

'I do not expect anything of value. I am only curious as to how the old people wrote their stories.' She pulled the look-see from her robes and placed in on the table. Her Matriarch's face twitched slightly, as if she recognised it.

'Read it to me,' Shayla implored.

Her Matriach sighed.

'You would not understand it,' she said. 'When you make *Majj*, you will learn to read. Keep the look-see until then.' Her Matriarch was referring to Shayla's impending maturity, at which time she would do pilgrimage across the Sahara desert, and at the temple in the Old Nubia she would be made a Matriarch.

But her *Majj* was centuries away yet.

'Will you not read it to me?' she implored again. 'At least tell me what it is about.'

Her Matriarch picked up the look-see and opened it.

'It is a story,' she said. 'Just like our legends, but older.'

Shayla leaned closer. 'What is it called?' she asked.

Her Matriarch flipped back to the cover and read its title out.

'The Holee Baybel.'

Shayla nodded, motioning for her to go on.

Her Matriarch flipped through the pages for a few moments, then shut the look-see firmly. 'I have read this story. It is one our own tales.'

'Really!' Shayla cried.

Her Matriarch nodded. 'It is about the fall of man. His deception by a dragon and his casting from Her grace. You know this story.'

From mother to daughter, gentle lies.

Shayla sighed. So the look-see was nothing new. It was the same old story she had heard as a girl, recycled over in this Holee Baybel. She stood up, trying to hide her disappointment. Her Matriarch stood too and pointed at the sun.

'Go to your husbands. They may not have the sense to put on their hats before She begins to rain. I will come to see Ateph before he passes.'

Shayla grasped her mother goodbye then left for the ranch.

The Matriarch stood by the doorway, watching her youngest daughter disappear into the purple haze that was the afternoon. She picked up the look-see, holding it a long time, feeling the weight of its history. After her *Majj*, Shayla would no doubt wish to read it. But before then it would do her no good. For in the look-see, as the Matriarch well knew, there were also tales of a woman named Eva. There were tales of a masculine God. Within many other look-sees too, there was testimony that nature had once held a different balance. At that time the feminine had not yet come to own the gift of long life by whatever science or magic the old people had possessed.

At that time men had been their equals.

At six hundred years of age, her daughter was much too young to understand such things. She would have to wait until she made *Majj*. The Matriarch placed the look-see carefully into an alabaster stone drawer, which she shut just as the Sun sighed in the sky and began to rain down Her gentle licks of blue purple fire.

The Bride

Tanya Chan-Sam

The wedding party was loud. Singing and dancing filled the yard outside. Neighbours from the surrounding farms sat on the stoep.

Sarah sat still on the bridal chair decorated with offerings from her kinfolk. She kept her eyes down, as prompted by her mother. An hour she'd been seated, her bottom feeling numb. The gaggle of conversation and laughter tormented her. She wanted to be outside, laughing with her cousins, sneaking a drink of beer. The mournful faces of the crying, female relatives around her seemed strange and scary. In her hands, she twisted a length of ribbon she'd pulled out of the hem of her dress. Her mother leaned over and grabbed it from her hand, bending down to rethread it through the hem. She said nothing, but placed a firm hand on Sarah's knee, willing her to sit still. Sarah twined her fingers together instead, playing 'Duimpie, duimpie se maat...' silently to herself.

On a corner table, the simple wedding gifts were piled. Mostly farm produce wrapped in cloth, one in heavy, brown paper wrapping, all illuminated by the paraffin lamp which had burned all day. Sarah swung her feet, trying to still the twitching in her legs. She'd heard so much about Meneer Jonkers, the farmer from across the valley. She knew he was older than she was, but had never met him. Everyone said how rich he was. Her mother had told her he had running water inside his house.

Darkness arrived and with it, Meneer Jonkers on his pony trap. The wedding party made two lines of back-slapping men and smiling women to hasten him to his new bride.

Sarah kept her eyes down, her heart racing, her fingers twined together, reciting in her head, 'Duimpie, duimpie se maat...' The wedding party was silenced by loud shushes from outside. Meneer Jonkers approached the bridal chair with care. He stood in front of her, held out his hand to Sarah. She placed her red knuckled hand on his; a crepe skin, ridged with prominent blue veins. He led her to the table where the wedding meal was spread. Fatty mutton stew plumped out with vegetables, cooked over the fires outside.

Meneer Jonkers was served first. He placed both elbows on the table and bent close over his steaming plate, his twitching nose and short eyelashes moving in his face as he absorbed the smells. Sarah watched him, her mouth opening to mirror his as he chewed the stewed meat. His chin, bobbing just like a piston, fuelled his open-mouthed chewing. It reminded her of oom Daan's old car, the engine guts laid bare, the pistons cranking up and down on their metal legs, devouring petrol and air, like Meneer Jonkers, compressing stew and air in his mouth.

Meneer Jonkers danced and sang on his wedding night. He clutched at Sarah, pressing his body into her breasts. She felt his hands pushing at her spine, his bearded jaw tickling and pricking her flushed cheek, his voice bass and hoarse, singing in her ear. He nuzzled at her hair. She heard him sniff. A sharp snort up his nose. Sarah wondered if he could smell the Sunlight soap she'd bathed in. She tilted her head towards his nose, hoping he would smell the rosemary water her mother had rinsed her hair with.

Meneer Jonkers left with his new bride at cock-crow, the dawn sky bruised purple with new light, their heads and shoulders dark silhouettes as they clip-clopped away on his pony trap. His house lay across the valley. A journey she'd never made.

True to her mother's words, he had running water in his house, a kitchen sink and bath in a bathroom. She followed him from room to room, open-mouthed. In the kitchen he asked her to light the fire, make a meal. She busied herself, relieved to have something to do after sitting still for so long.

They ate alone at the large table. He ate again with gusto, grinning at her. Sarah finished her meal before him and played 'Duimpie, duimpie se maat...' under the table.

Finally he pushed his plate away.

'Wil Meneer tee he?' she asked.

He smiled at her and nodded slowly: 'Ja, bring dit kamer toe.'

Sarah busied herself, cleaning the kitchen, polishing the dusty, coal stove.

'Sarah, wat maak jy?' he called from the bedroom.

'Ek kom, Meneer,' she called.

She turned the brass taps over the kitchen sink and water spouted out, warmed by the coal stove as he'd explained to her. She washed the two plates, holding out her hand in delight under the running water, then turned off the taps and started again.

'Sarah, wat maak jy?' he repeated from the bedroom.

'Ek kom, Meneer,' she called.

She searched for cups and saucers, a tray, sugar basin. Arranged them on the wooden tray covered with a beaded doily she found in a drawer filled with cloths and doilies. One for each day of the week. She traced the neat embroidery on their corners. Recognised 'Sondag' from the same letters she'd practised in Sunday school.

'Sarah, waar is jy?'

'Ek kom, Meneer.'

She tested the water in the copper kettle. She wondered if it was hot enough to be carried down the long passage to his bedroom. She'd never had to transport tea before. Surely the air would cool it; and Meneer Jonkers would not want a cold cup of tea. Back on the centre hot plate she moved the copper kettle. It had to be singing, her mother had said.

'Ek kom, Meneer,' she called before he asked again.

Every step down the passageway was carefully placed, her eyes wide, her hands gripping the tray, holding it tightly. Another few more steps. Not a drop spilled.

The door swung open. Meneer Jonkers stood on the threshold. Bare-arsed naked. Poedel-nakend. She must have fainted. The tray must have fallen. Meneer Jonkers must have tried to catch it and the hot-hot tea must have fallen on him, spilling over his pancake-flesh skin, the sparse, grey chest hairs turning orange as the hot, dark tea emptied onto him. His heart in his frail body must not have been able to withstand the shock.

Sarah arrived sweating and barefoot at her old home, her wedding dress dirty, the ribbon dangling around her knees. She cried and shouted at her bleary eyed mother:

'Toe ek wakkerskrik, le hy langs my, poedel-nakend en dood. Die Here weet hoe dit gebeur het. Die Here weet alleen.'

'When I woke up, he was lying next to me, poedel-nakend and dead. The Lord knows how it happened. The Lord only knows.'

The news must have grown wings, flown over the whole valley, because, by mid-afternoon, their stoep was again full of Jonkers relatives, looking solemn and in no mood for festivities.

'A charge must be laid.'

The Jonkers family nodded their heads in agreement. Their relative had to have justice.

Three months later in the District Circuit Court, which was held in the town hall, Sarah sat on the wooden chair she'd been escorted to. She could hear the sound of bodies moving behind her as the public filed in. The low hiss and murmur of dress fabrics and trouser material as thighs and bums sat down. The twisting of arms and backs as coats and jackets were removed. Sarah could hear whispered voices, low greetings, someone laughing. A voice called out for the windows to be opened to let in fresh air. The clerk rose from his seat. Sarah's head turned as her eyes followed him walking towards the tall windows of the town hall. A row of Jonkers relatives met her gaze. A clump of them reared in unison, shouting, 'Moordenaares!'

Sarah turned in panic, searching the rows of faces for her mother. She found her sitting upright in the middle of a row of female relatives; all were dressed in sombre black, staring ahead.

Sarah twisted back in her seat, placed her palms on her knees to stop them shaking. From the back of the court room a rumble of voices replied to the Jonkers family's outbursts.

'She's bleddy wel innocent!'

'Sarah Jonkers is a tragic young bride widowed on her wedding night. Have some pity!'

Sarah looked ahead to where the judge's table stood, the chair fitted neatly under the table, awaiting him. She kept her wide eyes on the judge's empty seat, twisting her fingers around themselves, quietly whispering, 'Duimpie, duimpie se maat, langeraat, fielafooi, pis innie kooi.' *Thumb, thumb's mate, the long one, the one next to the long one, piss in the bed.*

tell tales

Flight of Freedom

Courttia Newland

H is first inkling that something strange was happening came when he noticed an annoying itch on both shoulder blades. He, of course, was Marcus Jennings, your lower than average rude boy type who lived in the heart of the Inner City – you know, the type of kid Ali G made millions parodying. And the itch? Well, the itch was nothing special at the time. Not painful but deep, insistent. Not nagging for attention, but whining softly like a puppy left outside in the thick of winter. He noticed it most in the mornings, but found when he left the house and went outside, got into conversation with the mans dem in their usual spot, he could ignore the itch. Smoking weed and drinking Nigerian Guinness also helped. And as they stood on the corner and bus' jokes, sold overpriced skunk to the tourists and complained about the gentrification of what they had once known and loved, he forgot that he'd ever had itchy shoulder blades. Until he left the corner for his tower block home.

There, with his head spinning and only thick darkness to gaze at, the itch came back with a vengeance that had him rubbing his back against his mattress, making it impossible for him to sleep. Unable to appease or quiet the sensation, he often marched into the bathroom, grabbed his loofer, reached over his shoulder and attacked his blades until the skin was tender. He only stopped because the pain grew stronger than the itch. He downed two aspirins, smoked some skunk and prayed he'd drift away.

Two days later Marcus went to see his GP, Dr McBride, after it became clear that the itch wasn't going away. The doctor gave him a routine check up, took his blood pressure, gazed into his eyes with his little torch thingy, then pronounced that Marcus was in perfect health. He'd have to go to St Mary's for further blood tests, but the Doctor was pretty sure there was nothing to worry about really. When Marcus complained of feeling sore, McBride felt around his shoulder blades and put the tenderness down to all the scratching. On a whim, born mainly out of the fact that he was completely baffled by Marcus's so called 'ailment', the GP placed his stethoscope on the shoulder blades, shrugged at his patient (who was giving him a very strange look), then inserted his earpiece and listened. Later, Dr McBride told his wife that what he'd heard was the strangest thing he'd come across in twenty years of medicine. Low-pitched, steady crunching sounds, the kind cornflakes made if you took a handful and crushed them in your fist. It took all of his experience and training to keep his face neutral, not to panic when he heard those noises. *Why didn't you just tell him?* Mrs McBride had asked her husband, truly unable to fathom his motives.

I don't know – I just froze, the doctor replied, looking at the floor while his conscience reminded him, once again, that he was lying.

Dr McBride hadn't told Marcus because he didn't have a clue what was causing the noises – it was as simple as that. To admit that he didn't know something was near enough impossible for a man who always knew *everything*. So, the pride of Dr McBride – excuse the lame rhyme, I couldn't resist – saved Marcus from becoming some kind of medical oddity for the remainder of his natural life.

Because Marcus never went for his blood tests.

He had suspected something was badly wrong since the itching began, and when he saw McBride's rigid emotionless mask as he held the cold stethoscope and listened, intuition told him the doctor was hiding something. Which probably meant that what he had was very bad, maybe even terminal. Marcus went straight home that day, avoiding his usual corner with his usual bredrins and instead stopping off at the local Tesco's Metro to buy as many provisions as he could afford. If he was going to die, he would go out with a bang, he decided. He would experience everything he'd ever dreamed about.

Up until that point, Marcus's life had been a bit of a non-starter. He'd been average at school, far too average to be interested in college, opting for the brighter allure of street life. He'd tried selling various drugs, only to realise you had to be more than average at maths in order to make it worthwhile; and he, of course, was not. When he turned and looked around it had been ten years since he'd left school. He hadn't managed to gain anywhere near the amount of money it took to have the cars, women and respect that drugs were supposed to bring. He fell back on his giro, which meant that although he was handsome, he stopped attracting the type of women he dreamed of. As his confidence plummeted, he stopped attracting any at all.

Nowadays he stood on the corner selling the odd draw for other dealers, turning ten-pound bags into twenty and nicking a spliff when he needed it. Sometimes he remembered his former dreams of being someone big as he stood with the others, all pretending that they did this only to keep their area real, to prove they were still as hardcore and street as ever. The lie had never held much weight for Marcus. He still wanted something other than the life he'd been awarded but, much like his itch, he tried to pretend the feeling had never existed.

The itch soon gave way to a pain that had him running to the 24-hour store in the early hours of the morning, buying 6 packets of painkillers, going through three by the following night. Over the next week, sleep became a thought dreaded almost as much as death. It was impossible on his back. He turned onto his side or stomach, wincing in pain whenever he forgot and rolled over as normal. Though the drugs dulled his agony into a low-level hum, like the song said, they didn't quite work.

Then one morning, after going through the worst night of the lot only to fall asleep from sheer exhaustion, he opened his eyes to feel...nothing. The pain was gone. Yeah, he felt a little sore and tender, but that was minor compared to the howling agony he'd endured until now. Stunned, not quite believing the anti-climax of his troubles disappearing like a rainbow, he crept towards his full-length mirror, turned his back on the glass, and looked over his left shoulder.

There, reflected just below his incredulous face and the muscles of his neck, was a tiny, damp and fragile-looking wing. It was slightly bent over, limp as a plant's new shoot. It smelt musty, probably due to the wet feathers. The top half, the half nearest his chin, was grey, though the colouring faded into creamy white by the time it got to the tip of the wing.

Trembling, Marcus turned his head to the right and saw an identical twin, nestled in exactly the same spot. Emotion swelled inside him. He wondered if the wings could move. As he thought this, they flapped weakly in response. He gasped and tried again, laughing as it worked. It was as easy as moving his arm or fingers. Joy flowed through him until he was jumping on the spot, grinning from ear to ear, whooping loudly. *I've got wings*, he kept whispering under his breath. *Surely that means I can fly!*

How this miracle had happened he didn't know, much less care – but if he eventually might be able to fly, it obviously wouldn't be with those weaklings on his back. So he'd have to wait. Wait and see what happened.

It took twelve days for the weaklings to become strong, twelve days in which he continued avoiding the friends and dealers he'd once seen on a daily basis, even though they often came by his flat, demanding he let them in. Marcus refused. It wasn't that he was ashamed of his newfound body parts – far from it – but he knew as well as anyone what the manor was like. Once a person had wings everyone else would want them, wouldn't they? First, he'd be inundated with questions: *How did you get them? What did you do? How can I get them?* Then, when people realised he didn't know and couldn't help, admiration would turn to jealousy. And if he reacted badly that would be it. They'd seek a way to deal with him. That would definitely involve violence.

So Marcus hid.

That didn't mean he stayed away from everyone. Some nights he put on a raincoat and headed for the nearest park. When he got there, he took off the coat to reveal his bare torso, stretching his wings to the fullest. The only people in the park at that time were straight and gay lovers, and all were amazed by his mutation. Each wing was two feet long, growing stronger every day. Sometimes he'd flap hard enough to levitate a foot or so, though this brought a return of the pain and he didn't do it often. On every visit to the park the pain would lessen a fraction. By the end of the second week, it was gone.

One night, two Italian girls strolled past, hand-in-hand, making a beeline for Marcus. They'd heard, they told him. They were wondering...did he have any other amazing body parts?

By that time, of course, his secret was out. After the night with the Italian girls he'd been so pleased with himself he walked from the park to his home with his growing wings on display for all to see. He hadn't got far before a car steamed past, packed with four of the guys that he used to move with. Even though he'd known it was coming, the depth of their aggression still shocked him. They screamed, jeered and threw cans. Marcus didn't bother with a reply, flexing his angel-like wings instead. They were past six feet now, one of his park admirers had told him. If he wanted to get away from all he'd known, now was the time.

As he walked into his tower block lobby, stunning the security guard into a near fit, he knew they'd wait until he got inside his flat before they came. He had time. Once inside, he packed a small gym bag with essential items – his passport (he laughed at the sight of the little burgundy booklet, but took it anyway), a few clothes, a toothbrush, what little money he had and some favourite CD's. Then he opened his patio doors onto the outside world.

His flat was on the 14th floor of Trellick Towers. The tallest council block in Europe, let alone London. He'd been thinking about jumping since that first morning he looked in the mirror at himself, but had been too scared he might fall. Now, as he stared over his shoulder at the huge feathery appendages he'd grown, there was only anticipation – only joy. He could do it. He knew that he could, believed that he could. And if he couldn't, what else was there? Resign himself to a life where he had wings yet couldn't use them? A life as a chicken instead of an eagle?

He climbed up on the ledge and perched, like he'd seen birds do all his life, never knowing how long he'd wished their talents were his. When the shouting came he closed his eyes and relished the noise – it was the sound of victory, the sound of deliverance. There was pounding on the door, the steady thud of boots, then a crash and harsh breathing as they tumbled inside. He waited until they caught sight of him.

Without opening his eyes, he let himself go.

There was an instant rush of wind in his ears and the sound of his former friends' screams of shock, which eventually faded until all he could hear was the rapid beating of his heart. He waited as long as he could before he tilted the wings, his stomach churning in response as he levelled out, then climbed. Marcus opened his eyes to see the city – *his city* – new, fresh, and alive in a way it had never quite been. He imagined seeing the unexplored world beyond West London like this. The thought brought an effortless smile to his lips.

Day 15

Sharmila Chauhan

I lie in bed willing my pulse to slow down, but my heart just pumps faster, my brain overflowing with blood. I force my eyes to shut and my mind to surrender to the blackness. Diving into the middle of the bed, I curl up into a ball. Foetal position.

Om Om Om. I chant.

I can't go back to sleep.

Like a child on the eve of her birthday, I can only emulate slumber. My eyes snap open at every possible sound. Minutes pass as disjointed thoughts and dreams until, gradually, I give in to the uncontrollable rise of my consciousness.

Behind me I can hear the sound of water splashing in the bathroom. Of water as it pours over the body onto the bath... How many times have I heard the same sound as my mother, brother, father all took their morning baths? My mind rests on these childhood memories, sucking them like a lollipop, passing layer after layer of sweetness.

Those baths remained a fixture of my life until university, after which they were only reserved for holidays at home. That's where I met Suresh, the man in the bath. Tall, athletically built with skin the colour of browned herbs, he was my first love.

He is running the water now, warming the tub before he sits down, his face stern in concentration. I smile through my eyelids, remembering the pizza boxes, course notes and anatomy posters strewn across my room as he gradually moved into my flat. We were both twenty-one. It was easy then, simple. Love flowed between us with a deep, golden glow.

I doze off. Where did the time go? Next week I'll be thirty-five, the chances of a Downs child increased from 1/1600 to 1/370. I know this – the statistic from my university days comes to life like a resurrected skeleton.

He has turned the tap off. I can hear a sucking sound as water spins into the drain. A silence instead of water splashing against skin. I hear the familiar thud as the lota, our silver bowl, falls into the plastic bucket. Suresh has finished his bath. Rubbing himself down with body cream, he will be facing the calendar taped onto the bathroom door – temperatures, moods and menstrual cycles annotated across it in hopeless blue biro. Looking closer, his eyes squinting in the steam, he will see that today is marked with a big red ring.

I surface from the depths of the bed, like a whale coming up for air.

The morning stretches out with the tediousness of insomnia. After his bath, Suresh brings me a pot of tea. Sitting on the bed, he pours me a cup of the too sweet, fragrant liquid. Sipping it cautiously, I lean on the headboard and watch him get ready: attach his cufflinks, pull his tie, a little bit of wax through his hair, then a whisper of aftershave on his freshly shaved cheeks, a tender palm over the side of my face. Light lips brush my forehead, and he is gone.

I know he does not realise what he leaves me with. Of course, the cosy haven of our apartment is very real. The neatly organised kitchen, the washing machine humming with its early morning chore, the tidy shelves of our shared books, the bedroom with fitted cupboards and generous bed. Everything we could desire. Almost.

Tonight, if Suresh isn't too tired, I know he will run his smooth hands over my nighty, turn me around and make love to me. But these days there is only his pleasure, his climax, that counts. Only the filling of the dark, empty, unseen space...

It wasn't his fault. Although it was. Biologically. We both knew it. The doctors confirmed it. It was his sperm – those microscopic tadpoles with so much tenacity that they can stay alive inside a woman for forty-eight hours. Yes, they were there swimming in that pale white liquid that I had sucked off in my twenties, in the condoms I had flushed down the toilet and then, later, after marriage, inside me as I religiously took my pill...

Bitterness scratches my throat as I remember the 'scare'. I was twenty-four and a House Officer in the same hospital as Suresh. My best friend and I were on the same ward round.

'I can't believe I am doing this!' I called from the cubicle.

I ran my urine over a 'borrowed' test stick from the pharmacy as Kalifa waited by the door.

'Just do it and hurry up. We got ward round in ten minutes.'

'OK, OK! Eeww, I got it all over my fingers!'

'Come on, Nuray, its only urine. Hurry up... You done yet?'

'Yep... Hold on.'

'Come on, Nue, open the door.'

We pressed up against each other in the cubicle, arms and legs interlocking like two young giraffes.

'Oh my God, what if I am?'

'You're not! Don't worry, it's gonna be fine.'

I sat on the toilet, breathing deeply.

'Om, Om, Om.' I recited the mantra over and over again. 'Please God, don't let me be pregnant.'

'Shut up, Nue. How long has it been?'

We both peered at the long plastic stick on the floor.

'Seriously, Lefa, what am I gonna do if I am?' I jabbered like I was on death row, only a few minutes till my sentence was determined.

Kalifa was bent down, her bony bottom pressing into my stomach, deaf to my question. Her watch went off.

'It's negative...'

How I hugged her, smiled at my best friend's face, kissed her full on the lips.

'Thanks. Oh, thank God!'

Of course I wasn't. There was no way I could be.

Suresh has immobile sperm. This isn't the same as a low count. They are all there, like a classroom of children in reception; it's just that ninety per cent of them don't actually leave registration to go anywhere. They just sit there. Waiting.

I try not to get angry, but resentment fondles my heart like a lost lover.

Every Sunday, his mother lays a cold accusing hand on my stomach. It's always then that I look to Suresh, to those large hazel eyes for reassurance. But he is silent, leaving my empty womb to make its own excuses.

Meanwhile, my eggs are ripening, only to fall into an empty void.

Was it the oestrogen-tainted tap water that he consumed? Or perhaps the tight trousers? That time I took the pill for too long? Was I all there?

But I had seen it, this womb of mine, in scans. Different colours whirring around the cavity like aliens. I feel it too, alive and angry as it pulses monthly, wringing out my deep red lining and empty egg.

Those times are the worst. The few days beforehand Suresh is a nervous wreck, constantly looking into *my* face for reassurance. Constantly watching my movements to see if I reach for *that* box in the bathroom. When it comes, my back tender, stomach swollen, blood dripping between my legs like an angry wound, neither of us can say a word.

'We can adopt...' he used to say into my hair, cradling me before we had the tests. At that time I was terrified it would be my fault, that his mother was right. That maybe he would be justified in leaving me as I couldn't fulfil my side of the bargain. Now I wonder if I would be equally justified in leaving him...

No. I can't leave my husband with his hairy nostrils, the scar running up his leg from a bike accident, the man who laughs at me when I get drunk on a glass of wine, who strokes my head in the morning, wraps me in his arms at night. No. I can't. No matter how deep this longing. And I could. Men do it all the time, that or take up another wife. Everyone does it. Is union irrelevant if you can't procreate? Are we such animals? Apparently so.

Would he have an affair though?

My heart beats faster. Or would I take a child ripened by another woman, that grew inside her for nine months? No, I wouldn't. I couldn't. Rather be alone.

I turn around, facing the ceiling, suddenly feeling very hot. I kick the duvet off. The hot air rises away from my body like a balloon.

It's afternoon. My bag is packed with house-keys, purse, lipstick, perfume and book. A cold sweat rests on the back of my neck. I loiter at the front door until the last possible minute then, when it's nearly too late, I run out the door.

'Dr Aurora!'

It is Mr Aziz, my neighbour, smiling around his front door.

'Hello!' I call back over my shoulder.

'How are you?' A whiff of afternoon Indian cooking washes down their driveway.

'And Dr Aurora?' He grins, enjoying this moment.

'Fine too.' I unlock the car door.

'Good, good. Our two doctors are fine! Now I know you are very busy children...Come later if you want food, you know your Kaki always makes too much...'

'Yes, thank you.' My palms press together in a Namaste.

'OK, good, good.'

'I have to go. I'm going to work...'

I hesitate over the car roof. That final moment. Hoping he will detain me.

'OK, OK, beta. I won't keep you.' He smiles with a pride worthy of a father.

'OK, thanks, Kaka. Bye.'

I open the door and get in.

The journey is short. The clinic lies, inconspicuous, alongside a row of terraced houses. I wait outside, running the engine. He is already there on the corner. Grinning, he takes a final puff of his cigarette and walks over to the car.

'Hello.' His lips meet mine as he slides in next to me smelling of smoke.

It is always the same.

I drive around the back of the building, parking a few doors down. There is a slamming of doors in unison, shy smiles and the unlocking of a front door. There, without a moment to spare, I press myself onto him. His fingers reach into my hair; his tongue tickles my neck as his lips search me out until I give in.

He lifts my breasts out of his favourite pink lace bra. I roll my knickers down to my ankles. There is a bed. Pushing me down on all fours he parts my cheeks; he eases a hand in between, muttering pleasure when he finds moisture. I lean forwards as he pulls my hair. I feel him rubbing inside me as I push back onto him, harder, clenching my fists, one hand holding onto my matrimonial necklace.

He thrusts hard. Opening my legs wider I give him full access, holding him inside to the point of pain. The afternoon light blinks into our makeshift bedroom. For a moment I stare outside, watching the outlines of people passing by. Suddenly he climaxes and falls back onto the mattress. I remain totally still, allowing everything to be absorbed inside me.

The steam glazes the mirror with a thin coat of white. I hear the front door open. It is Suresh. As I rise up from the pool of warmth, water falls away from my body, leaving me covered in damp freckles. I pull the towel around my waist. Standing there, a salty wetness covers my cheeks and runs down the back of my throat. I look up and scornfully acknowledge the calendar. There, encircled in red, Suresh has marked Day 15 – Ovulation Day.

Catching Pheasants

Manzu Islam

We were strangers in a small provincial English town. But we liked the town, its rows of white Georgian houses with dense hedges, its wide avenues with chestnut trees, and its parks with lakes. We loved the hills and the murmuring of beech forests we thought we heard from the edge of the town. Most of all we loved the fields in the valleys and the mud roads that meandered through their green expanse. Somehow they reminded us of the fields that we knew. Long ago, before we came to England. But Dulu and I didn't go there much. In these solitary spaces we felt exposed.

It wasn't that people were unfriendly. On the contrary, the ramblers were only too keen to greet you with smiles, though we didn't see much of the farmers. On the rare occasions when we ventured beyond the town, we would wonder about the well-cultivated fields.

No one would be tilling the land or reaping the harvests. We would look at each other and wonder by what miracle these fields became so abundant with crops. Everywhere you looked you saw evidence of human hands at work: the well-ordered fences, the ditches, and the planned wilderness of bushes. Yet we hardly ever saw anyone working on them. But we didn't go there much; perhaps that's why.

We stayed mainly in the town. Dulu worked in the kitchen and I served. People in this town liked curries and we were the only Indian takeaway, so we were busy. We didn't see the owner much either. He only showed up during the weekends to lend a hand and gather the takings, but we didn't mind being left alone. In fact, we were very happy to cook, clean and serve on our own.

Once we had closed up, we would sleep side by side in the upstairs room. On that night, like so many others before, I was tired after a long day and was drifting into sleep. It annoyed me when Dulu struck a match to light a cigarette. I said, What you doing, Dulu? But he stayed silent for a while, puffing away. I saw the glow fluttering in the dark. He said, B*osom friend*, and paused again. Dulu always called me *bosom friend*. He addressed me that way even when he was cross with me.

– What is it, Dulu? I asked.

– I want to catch some of the pheasants, he said.

I laughed, thinking it was yet another of his crazy ideas, and like all his crazy ideas would die a slow death in the next few days.

– How you plan to catch pheasants, Dulu? I asked.

He reminded me of the little stream that we discovered one afternoon, last autumn, when between opening and closing time we had, quite by chance, ventured into the beech forest. There we had seen hundreds of pheasants moving in concord with the colours that cascaded from the canopy above. For a long time, taking cover behind a blackthorn thicket, Dulu and I had watched them.

Suddenly, as if to shake the enchantment out of us, Dulu asked me if I knew that pheasants originally came from the Indian sub-continent. I said I knew that.

– Look how natural they look in this place, he said. Like they've always belonged here.

– Yes, Dulu, I said. That's why people see them as the most English of all birds.

We often thought of returning to that place to see pheasants, but our courage usually failed us. We had managed only a single visit since then. Now, hearing of Dulu's dream of catching pheasants, I reminded him that the place was private, that you needed a licence to catch them.

– We need no licence, he said. We'll go after the closing time and just catch one.

– We might get into trouble, Dulu.

– What trouble, *bosom friend*? Have you ever seen a soul around there?

I waited for the idea to die down, but Dulu wouldn't let it go. One night, after closing time, the cleaning done, we set off for the beech forest in Dulu's old Renault. It took us only a few minutes to leave the lights of the city behind. It was a dark night and an autumnal chill had set in. We entered the open country, passing villages deep in their solitary dreams, our headlights momentarily outlining the hills as we turned bends. We parked near a hedge from where a path led down to the valley. We wrapped ourselves well, torches in hand, and took the path, walking light as we were carrying neither traps nor guns. I asked Dulu how he meant to

41

catch a pheasant. He said, Wait, *bosom friend*, you'll see.

We could barely make out the tracks with our torchlight. From all sides, beyond our little pool of light, darkness lay in ambush to claim us. Dulu, sensing my unease, reassured me that he had imprinted the layout of this land on his mind from our last visit. He could find his way even with the torches off. We crossed the valley, over a fence, and entered the beech forest down a sloping path. We walked on fallen leaves, but enough of them remained on the branches to murmur in the wind.

Dulu located the stream and we followed it. We knew that we had only to go down a few hundred metres, then across a fence to a clearing, and we would find a large gathering of pheasants. Already we could hear them rustling among the fallen leaves and undergrowth.

When we arrived at the clearing, our torches pointed, we saw hundreds of them milling in clusters. Our presence didn't seem to disturb them. Dulu said he would crawl near them, his torch off, and just grab one. He knew how to grab wild things, he said, as he had done so many times before coming to England. He had even grabbed poisonous snakes with his bare hands.

As I waited, leaning against a beech tree, Dulu went crawling in the darkness. He must have been at the point of leaping on one of the clusters when we heard a gun go off and the barking of dogs. The pheasants whipped up a storm as they scattered blindly. Dulu ran back and dragged me deeper into the forest. In the distance we could see light jerking between tall beech trunks. Amidst the barking of the dogs, another shot went off. No doubt they were looking for us. I held onto Dulu and he broke into a trot.

We didn't make any noise as the low branches sprang to whiplash us, their thorns cutting into our flesh. In our urgency to get away from the men and their dogs, we brushed past many beech trunks, though we didn't hit one head-on: it seemed Dulu knew his way in the dark. We climbed a slope, hurried down it, then climbed another. The dogs seemed to have the measure of us and were barking from nearer and nearer. Now we could even hear the men whistling as they directed them. I didn't know what Dulu was thinking, but I imagined the shock of the men as they beamed their torchlight onto us: two brown faces in the middle of an English wood. Surely it would have been the last place they expected to see the likes of us.

Sensing that the dogs were gaining on us, we made a frantic run. Luckily, we were already out of the woods and into a clearing. Dulu said, panting, I don't want to be taken alive, before we rolled down a giant slope. We were thrown into the air like bouncing balls and were battered, but got down with our limbs unscathed. We could still hear the dogs barking. At the foot of the slope we found the stream and waded through it, on and on until we couldn't hear them anymore. We dragged ourselves onto the land and lay there for an hour or so. Not a star to offer us a glint of light. The forest was silent again except for the murmuring of leaves. It was time to get back except, to our surprise, as we put our torches on we saw a cluster of pheasants dozing nearby. Before I could blink, Dulu made a lunge like a wild cat and caught one.

It seemed we had gone further away from our track than we thought we had, but Dulu took us back to the car. He put the pheasant in the boot and drove us back to our place.

– What are we going to do with the pheasant, Dulu? I said.

– Why, said Dulu, we're going to eat it. I'll cook something nice.

Dulu tied the pheasant's legs together with a string and put it on the kitchen's lino. It stayed quiet, although from time to time it would flap its golden wings.

– It looks so beautiful, I said.

– Yes, *bosom friend*, beautiful, said Dulu.

– Isn't it strange that his ancestors should came from the same place that we did? I said.

– Why, *bosom friend*, said Dulu, that's why he looks so beautiful. He's our country brother, isn't he?

– Should we kill him? I said.

– Don't be soft, *bosom friend*, said Dulu. Of course, we should kill him. He is meat, isn't he?

– Can't we keep him as a pet, Dulu? I said.

– How come you're becoming so English, *bosom friend*? Why make all that effort to catch good meat and fish to let them go? It's just stupid.

Dulu took a large knife from the drawer and I went up to clean my wounds and have a shower. I came back after twenty minutes and looked through the chink in the door. Dulu was sitting hunched over the pheasant which, I was surprised to see, was still alive. Suddenly Dulu got up with the knife and sharpened it with a flurry of jabs. He went around the room, muttering to himself, and then sat hunched over the pheasant again. He ran his finger over its long tail, as if trying to etch it in his memory, then got up again, this time grabbing the pheasant by the throat before going to the kitchen sink. He held its flapping wings between his legs and pulled its neck over the sink. When he lowered the knife I thought it was the end of the bird; but instead he threw the knife into the sink, laid the pheasant on the floor again, and lit a cigarette. As Dulu began to hum a tune I hadn't heard him humming in ages, I went quietly up to bed and lay there, thinking that Dulu hadn't the heart to kill the bird and how we could keep it as a pet, perhaps building a coup at the back.

I stayed in bed for an hour or so, waiting for Dulu to come. I wanted us to sleep as we always did, next to each other, Dulu lighting his last cigarette and telling me: *Bosom friend*, dream like a rainbow. When Dulu didn't come, I went down to the kitchen.

The pheasant lay in the sink in a pool of blood, its throat cut, its dark glassy eyes catching light from a ring of amber.

I said, What did you have to kill the pheasant for, Dulu?

Dulu didn't answer me. He was stroking the pheasant's feathers, their mirrors of rainbow, and had drifted into another world.

For Souhaité

Heather Imani

I have not survived my son. I dead inside. I never had a stillborn, but so it woulda feel, I sure. Souhaité is the second son I lose. Him get kill because he avenge his senior brother, Aimé, who – Lord forgive me – was no good. Generations my family and my husband family never involve in blood debt. Is why my father betroth me to Pious. Our family pride was that we stay outside of it. Even when people beg us to settle dispute because we impartial, we don't. Only once we intervene, when a child life was at stake.

The sky red and purple and black that day. They call me for Souhaité. When I go, I see him, twisting in the dry dirt. Every twist he make bruise up my body. I see death in his eyes. Death and surprise. That look on his face I carry before my eyes every God day since. And every night. If I don't dream how I meet him there in the dirt, I don't feel right in my spirit the next day. I need to remind myself how he was the day I lose him.

That day, I throw myself in the dirt too, red up all my clothes. The boys who came to call me look away. A senior woman like me, they must be thought I would be more dignify. I throw myself down and I hold him, squeeze him tight. I start sing the songs I used to hush him with when he was a baby. He smile, but fear deep in his eyes. I whisper, *N'aie pas peur, Souhaité, don't fear*...I sing the words to the baby-song tune. I wash his face with my tears. And I squeeze him. Squeeze him. To tell the truth, I want to press out from him what life he have left because the fear in his eyes coming like it going to mad me.

When he stop move, I wipe blood from his face with my scarf and I call to the boys. I turn my back while they lay him out straight and place his gun in his hand. I stop my ears while they walk around him and sing. After, I am supposed to give the command for when to raise him from the earth and carry him back to the house. Instead I scream a curse at them all. The one who has killed my son cannot look at me and that's how I know who he is.

Aimé. Is him first bring gun into our house. He wanted always to run with older boys in our area, break house and steal car, those kind of things. Is not one and two time I go to the police myself but they don't have much powers against these criminal boys. So all I beg the police, they just leave Aimé to this bad influence. Pious was sick that time, so he couldn't do much. He try to talk to Aimé, but by then Aimé well past listening. The glamour of the badness shining in his eyes make him blind, and the blindness affecting his ears make what his father say he can't hear.

Then one morning in the kitchen, I hear Aimé talking to Souhaité about how he been done an 'offence'. My blood freeze over the whole of my body, for I know is how these feud start. I ask is who could do him any offence? He tell me, all boasty in front of Souhaité, that he been seeing this woman... That is all I hear. *Offence over woman?* I ask him. *Boy, is mad you turn mad since you leave your bed?* He look at me like he don't know me and laugh. Same time, I wondering if I know who he is at all, because I can't see is the same boy I did born. So we both standing there, like strangers, looking in each other face. I send Souhaité out, tell him leave his breakfast and go to school early. He is like a sponge, and this is one thing I don't want him soak up.

After that, I just waiting for news.

I never actually get any news, but I see how people start to look at me, out the side of their eye. They ask after Aimé with acid edge in their voice – how they haven't seen him in however long. They know he stuck up in the house, can't go anywhere because he bring blood debt on his head – on our family head – over this woman who he never see fit to bring home but bring him to feel he have 'offence' to rectify. Until Aimé say one day he going out. Say he going mad stick up in the house and he will take his chances. Same time he step out is same time they get him.

After that, every day somebody ask me: *When will Souhaité act? When he going to act?* Every asking make my womb seize, like I have birth pain for Souhaité all over again.

Poor Souhaité. He start looking like donkey overladen. He don't care for sweets anymore or the cakes I bake that he used to love. Just barely eating. He looking hollow-out and I say I will take him to doctor but really I know what wrong with him. Worse, boys at school calling him coward (I never know this then) and then I adding to it (I never know this either) because I go into the square and preach against blood debt and shouting that I don't want my son death avenge, that a mother must admit when her child wrong and Aimé was wrong, and is God's will that he get take the way he did. Souhaité getting pressure because it look like his mother deciding whether blood debt get pay or pardon.

I beg Pious to speak out at the time, call a meeting of men with the other family and pardon the debt officially. But since Aimé get kill, it's like Pious own self collapse into nothing. Everything he used to be and stand for just fade off into dust, like moth wing. Pious did love Aimé too-too much. I always say so. Is dangerous for a man to love so. So Pious don't have no words for anybody but God. Day and night, he praying. Questioning God. But God not answering on how Pious supposed to proceed or help his family in this thing. So he stop. He stop doing anything. Until his sickness just sweep him up, and he going down, down – and he can't do nothing anyway after that.

Meantime, Souhaité getting jab-jab at school, until he box up right in a corner. One day, I come home from market to see the floorboard dig up. Now, I never know that anything under any floorboard. But soon as I see it, I know is where Aimé used to hide his things – gun, money, drugs or whatever else he might have get when he running with those boys. A note leave on the kitchen table that Aimé write to Souhaité the day he get kill, saying how Souhaité will never be a man if he don't avenge him, *if anything, the worst, should happen*, he write. So written, so it come to pass.

As my poor, break-down, only remaining son gone to avenge his no-good brother, same time they kill him back. He don't even get his customary amnesty to find compensation. (Nobody came to offer compensation for Aimé; I woulda take the money to release the debt and then burn it same time, right in front of them.)

Is little-little I notice. First, things move from where I put them. A dish, or some utensil. Always things that I have to do with. Pious never have anything he put down somewhere and then can't find. Is only when Souhaité picture crash down from the wall that I count back and see that it all begin thirty days after he get kill. That confirm what my mind telling me: Souhaité spirit don't settle into the dead world. After he break he own photograph, is pure smash, he start smash things in the house: glass, plate, window, plant pot – anything. I telling Pious that Souhaité not cross over properly, that he vex and he want something. Pious don't hear anything, don't see anything break – but by now, he living in his own head and he not giving me any strength.

I beg God take my son properly, rest his spirit down. Or, failing that, to take me or Pious so we could show Souhaité the way, for he hovering and that is not right. Same prayer I pray, over and over. Pray until I shake, until I bawling like baby want a feed. All the while, Souhaité breaking whatever he can as fast as it repair or replace, and I trying, trying to coax his spirit. I leaving his favourite cake, the sweets he used to like. But the more I leaving the sugarings, is the more Souhaité vex. He flinging down the Bible off the low table; he tearing up my good linen tablecloth. I fix, he break. I mend, he tear. Pious not able to help. His soul dark now. Myself, I feeling weigh down, like is rock-stone I have tie up in my belly. I stop go to church, for my foot feeling so leaden, they can't make the journey. Pious ailing bad but hanging on instead of letting go and make his spirit lead Souhaité spirit home – and that vexing me too.

One evening, when Souhaité set to chopping up the house again with his ghost machete, I go into the yard and I fling myself down in the dirt. This time, I cry out to Souhaité, not God – for God gone deaf long time to

me and Pious it seem. I chanting over and over, *Souhaité,*
que veux-tu? Hm? Is what you want mama do? I out
there from when the sun go down – that's six – until
must be midnight, twisting up in the dirt, redding up
my clothes again but I don't care. Is only when I tired
out and about to drop sleep right in the yard that I
notice the house all quiet. I thinking maybe Souhaité
tired out too, or maybe he feel sorry for me to see how
I distress so bad.

Next morning, I get up and start sort out what and
what will need to fix this time. Is then that I notice,
when I turn and see the yard where I was lying down,
the letters mark out in the red dirt. I put the letters
together and they make two simple words.

AVENGE ME.

I never even consider to tell Pious.

The rock-stone in my belly start to lift away and I
get myself ready quick-quick and straighten up the
place. I start to sing. Since I sing to Souhaité in the
dirt, I don't sing nothing – not even when I was still
going church. Now, I singing Souhaité lullaby. Soft at
first, then loud. Pious don't call to me though. My hands
doing all different jobs, quick-quick: mend, fix, clean,
replace, repair. Then my foot carry me to the yard, to
the garbage drum. I know it have in broken glass but
my hand just plunge in – no cut up – and pull out the
gun that been there since those killer boys place it in
Souhaité hand and carry him back to the house with it.
When he did reach, I pull the gun from his hand and
fling it in the garbage. It been there ever since. Now
my hand draw it out and I holding it. I put on my shoes,
and I gone.

Is true that the weight in my belly was lifting off
since I read Souhaité message – but is only when I shoot
the boy who couldn't look at me that day, is only when
I shoot him outside the school that he and Souhaité

attend, that my body start feeling light, like I soaring, like I high.

The sky so clear. The sun throwing its heat pretty, not fierce. No cloud in the heavens. Air fine, pure, sweet – like the sea nearby, only we don't have no sea by us. I know I must be walk home, but it seem like the sweet air just carry me, for I don't feel no effort of walking.

When I get home, I know Souhaité angry spirit gone at last. Is only light around the house, even in all the corners. But something else too: Pious gone. His spirit not present in the house anymore – I feel it. Is only then I realise. Pious must have pass over last night, when I was twisting up in the yard. That is why, when I get up, the house already calm. Why he not calling to me when I singing loud-loud this morning. I also realise that if Pious pass over last night to show Souhaité spirit the way home, then the message I read in the dirt next morning was old, like overnight food.

But it too late now. I done shoot the boy outside the school already.

Now my breath start feeling short, hard to get out past my throat. I holding off the rock-stone that trying to invade my belly again, my chest, my soul. No, I staying light. I staying soaring. I staying swimming in pure, sweet air, like sea air (although no sea is by us) because I see those two simple words mark in the red dirt. What my poor son ask me, I do for him. Like any mother would who distress bad-bad as I was. He ask me. And what he ask me, I do. For Souhaité.

Breakfast Time

Leone Ross

Tina wakes up at 6.30 to take out the earplugs. Pink lilies rustle at the window; someone has forgotten to close it and cold air loops through. She reaches up to tuck the urine-coloured blanket around her left shoulder. Everything hurts. Hospital wards are noisy, especially at night. The nurses try to speak in low voices but low voices are unnatural and so they succumb to failure and rebellion. The woman lying in the bed next to her is called Rose. She specialises in theatrical moans and complaint. She forgets that she can shit where she lies, into a special bag made for that purpose, so she yells for a nurse whenever she feels the urge, even at 2 a.m.

Tina hates Rose and wishes she would die. Tina presses the call button when she needs a nurse and when they come at night she whispers at them. A man yells in the ward next door: he sounds drunk. A nurse speaks to him. She is professional. She sounds as if someone has slipped razor blades into her voice. The man calls her a nurse cunt. There is a bang and a squawk. Tina's eyes widen. A male nurse runs up the hallway and there are scuffling sounds. Rose sleeps on, her toothless mouth a slackened 'O' shape. Nothing disturbs her when she is asleep. The scuffles die down. The drunk man is promising to behave, only that it huuurts, it huuurts.

Tina watches Rose smile in her sleep. Rose has no teeth, but when the physiotherapists walk her around the ward in the morning, her back is straight, her belly flat, and her smile imperious. She has the carriage of a withering dancer. Tina reaches down for her stitches and thinks that she will look like Rose soon. She smiles.

Belly. It has not cost her lovers or work. She confounds men and theatre critics, which is to say she confounds most men. She has made it her mission to distract them from her imperfection, and so critics speak of her unexpected Desdemona and the soaring energy of her Abigail Williams and lovers handle her body with suspicion and awe and casual words:

'You are quite beautiful, you know. And onstage...yes.'

What they mean is fat and what they mean is that they cannot forget the fat and what they mean is they enjoyed her despite the fat.

The fat will be gone soon.

The ward stirs. Breakfast is imminent. A nurse says good morning and asks if Tina needs pain relief. Yes. Morphine, as always. She likes it. It is a pretty, smooth high and all she needs to do for more is demand it. She rolls over and the nurse points the needle at the big muscle in her ass, below the hip.

'A sharp scratch,' she warns.

Tina wriggles her toes as the needle goes in, then presses and rubs the sting. She remembers the first morphine, the day after surgery. Blurred eyes, lying, giggling, looking at the other patients. Old women, but changed by the drug into strange objects. A huge peach pit. A crumpled piece of newspaper. Rose was a lobster shell. Tina lay for an hour, looking at them, singing under her breath.

Above the bed, she is named and defined: Tina Bernard. Nil By Mouth, which means no food, no drink. Her mouth is dry. She has not eaten for two days. She is always conscious of the cannula in the back of her left hand, its plastic needle buried into the vein, lacing away from her towards a beeping machine. The drip makes her feel like a real patient, like the people in movies and hospital TV shows. She has to take it to the bathroom with her, rolling it across the floor, tucking it in beside her as she lowers haunches to toilet.

The cannula doesn't hurt, but it is alien and she fears her sleeping movements will dislodge it. It only lasts a day at a time, any longer and her wrist balloons then hurts, her body rejecting the invader. Nurses move over her, tutting and comforting, to remove it. 'My, you're sensitive,' one says. But she likes the cannula. The saline feels cold and thin in her veins and it makes her pee in waterfalls.

She snakes her right hand down her swollen abdomen. The surgeon says there will be minimal scarring and that makes her want to laugh, and then to hide, thinking of him poring over her belly, snipping, tying off, whatever surgeons do. He will have seen that one more scar will make no difference, will be lost between the stretch marks, ripples, bulges. She remembers the face of the GP who suggested surgery, how angry she was, and the righteousness of her girlfriends – how dare he, she must report him, for insensitivity, for political incorrectness, for something.

And then, a month ago, lying in a deep bath, she regards the belly. She has spent years pretending it isn't there. She has learned how to dress, to make love, to dance, to take the stage in ways that hide it from herself. But now she sees. It curves above the water, a bulbous, horrid thing. She closes her eyes and tries to make it beautiful: apricot-coloured, glowing in the light. She fails.

She has done this alone. No one knows she is here.

She dozes. The ward lights brighten and nurses bustle. Breakfast is served at 7.30 a.m. but she has been nil by mouth for two days and the orderlies wheel the food trolley past her, yelling at the old women stirring:

'Cereal, Mrs. Brown. Do you want cereal? Cornflakes? Porridge? Tea, Mrs. Brown? No, tea! Do you want tea?'

It has been splendid to fast, to feed on salt water and morphine. Starvation is sweet and new. Each breakfast time she prays she will be missed again; if they come to her with food she fears she will scream – she doesn't want them adding worry to her chart. She reads the chart to see what they say about her. Patient is independent. Patient asked for pain relief. Patient read for several hours and slept well. She has been a good girl. She does not want them to give her a bad report card. But last night, new joy. A memory that she is safe. They have clamped her inside. Two ounces, they say. That's all you'll hold. She imagines days of choosing carefully: beautifully whipped mashed potatoes, one spoon, two spoons, done; a celery stick that fills her up; a meal of freshly squeezed orange juice.

Victory.

A nurse pats the blankets around her and says her name. She unscrews the looping, plastic drip. The beep cuts out, like someone died.

'I have a surprise for you,' says the nurse. 'Today you get breakfast. Won't that be nice? Then you can have a nice wash and a walk, eh?'

Tina smiles. She is ready.

It has been twelve days. Tina disturbs the patients at night; she cannot stop crying. The nurses are worried and they speak to her at all hours, matter-of-fact or sweet as lilies, like razor blades or ticking watches: nothing changes anything. There is talk of moving her somewhere else.

She cannot eat because the food will not stop speaking. That first breakfast, a cup of clear soup that chattered down her throat. It talked about architecture: panelling, refurbishment, ceiling structure. When she swallows the voice stutters, like a damaged CD player. The single teaspoon echoes in her tiny stomach, the voice half a second behind the primary voice that rambles in the cup before her, an irritating, doubling effect that makes her head swim. She vomited then, weak and surprised. The nurses said this was ordinary and that she shouldn't worry, but she does. At luncheon, more food spoke. An orange on a nearby table hummed a reggae song. Raspberry jam laughed at her as it disappeared down ill, wrinkled throats. She tries to tell the doctors that she cannot eat, that things have changed, but they look at charts and they look through her and they tell her about case studies.

'Calm down,' one says. She is Roman-nosed, slender. Looks as if she's smelled something bad.

Tina stares at a quarter of a mashed banana on the tray before her. She wants to eat it, but it is reciting the alphabet in patient, liquid tones. The spoon beside it begins to vibrate.

'COMRADES!'

A cup across the room:

'COMRADE?'

'WELCOME TO OUR THIRD ANNUAL GENERAL MEETING, COMRADES! JOIN ME WHILE WE SING! ARISE, YE SOLDIERS OF ALL NATIONS...'

'CONDEMNED TO MISERY AND WOE!'

'TO HELL WITH HUMBLENESS AND PATIENCE!'

'GIVE DEADLY BATTLE TO THE FOE!'

Their voices rise shrilly. The fork beats time. A pat of butter purrs. The mashed banana begins the nine times table. A breadcrumb squeaks. Rose stares at her, her mouth an old 'O' shape.

Tina is screaming.

She is losing weight.

tell tales

Stain Removal

Emily Pedder

It was the night of Live Aid and a bunch of us were round at Elvira's house because her parents were away, and besides they were hippies so what did they care. And Elvira had some home-grown – her very own batch – which she said was really strong and pure and *buddy*; which I didn't understand but nodded as if I did. And she had these super king-size rainbow Rizlas that her and Zac had bought when they went to Amsterdam instead of going on the school trip to Lyme Regis like everyone else. And Elvira skinned up a big joint, and I mean big because she licked three of the papers together and built a giant reefer for everyone to share. And she passed it round while we watched Bob Geldof on the TV talking about starving kids in Africa, and people lay on her mum's embroidered cushions and we all said how pure the weed was and Elvira smiled, like she knew. And I wanted to say how stoned I was but no one else did and I didn't want to

61

look like an idiot because I'd only just scraped an invite by the skin of my teeth. And these lot were cool. I'd been trying to be cool for months, the kind of cool that doesn't try to be cool, it just is; that was what I wanted. I knew I wanted it, I just didn't know how to get it, so I really didn't want this to fuck up. And Nina, who had come with me (although I was already starting to wish she hadn't because even though Nina was my best friend, she just didn't look right there, didn't have the right air about her – not like Elvira or Zac or any of the others at the party who just looked naturally cool, like they were born that way), well, Nina was drinking from this bottle of vodka – and no one else was really drinking, so that made her stand out in the first place, and she was getting drunk and laughing and being stupid and I wanted her to stop because that wasn't the right vibe, but she didn't realise. And next thing I know she's disappeared out of the room with this tall man, and I'm left alone. And I waited for her and bit my nails and tried not to look like a spastic. And Elvira talked about how rubbish the Moroccan was last year and how the best puff she'd had recently was the Thai stick her dad brought her back from holiday. And I sat on my nails so I wouldn't bite them and wished Nina would come back because no one was talking to me – no one even seemed to know I was there – and my clothes were all wrong and I wished my Mum and Dad were hippies and knew about cool things like weed and Thailand. And about half an hour later – although it felt like three years – Nina came back, and she was smiling and sauntering into the room like the cat who's got the cream. And the tall man appeared, except I saw then that he wasn't a man; he was a boy, a tall boy, thirteen – like us (well fourteen, *actually*). Nina told me later like that was something to brag about which, of course, it was. And

Nina sat down next to me and that's when I noticed her trousers were on the wrong way round, and there was this damp mark near the pockets which were inside out. And then I realised other people had noticed too because I could hear the whispers and the sniggers and I knew this definitely wasn't going to go down as cool. And I said let's go to Nina and she shrugged and said okay – because Nina is like that – and I got up and walked out of the room and Nina followed and I prayed no one noticed she was with me (although I knew they did). And outside she said what's the hurry. And I said your trousers are on inside out. And she laughed and said so they are, and then she looked at me, all mysterious, in a way I hadn't seen before. And I said why. And she said tall boy/man had *licked her out* and she must have put them on wrong. And I felt a rush of blood to my cheeks and thought they were going to burn off. And I said you're a slag. And she said takes one to know one, although that was a load of rubbish because she knew I'd never done anything like that before. And then I saw Elvira's face at the window and she was looking at me through the glass and pointing and I swore her and Zac were laughing. And I said let's just catch the night bus home. And Nina said okey dokey. And we walked to the bus stop and I knew then and there I'd never get onto the cool list and I'd probably never be invited to one of Elvira's parties again. And to be honest, that seemed like the end of the world.

It was the afternoon of the Art class and me and Nina were sitting in the portacabin, which is where they had the art classes when the other building got checked for asbestos. And Mr Roberts put a goat's skull and an old bit of wood in the middle of the table. And the room smelled of BO from the last class, and Mr Roberts's cheese and onion pasty. And Mr Roberts was talking about textures and tones and contours, or some such rubbish, but I wasn't listening because I was looking at Rachel Benson who was picking her nose and actually eating it. And Mr Roberts said we could start drawing, so everyone picked up their charcoal while Mr Roberts circled the room and said things to people in his low voice: *that bit could do with being a bit darker; don't be afraid to be bold; really focus* – stuff like that. And Nina was busy drawing really fast because she's brilliant at Art, so good she can actually make things look like they really do. And every time I looked at hers I felt sick because I knew mine was shit and the skull looked like it was floating in the middle of nowhere and the wood looked like a wrinkly turd. And when we'd finished Mr Roberts held up Nina's drawing and said this was a great example of a *lively, well-balanced, acutely-observed still life*. And Nina purred because she loves Mr Roberts, who is one of those teachers that's old but young: he's got grey hair but he wears jeans, and he still listens to pop music. (And he smokes too: one time me and Nina saw him round the back of the portacabin having a fag and he offered us a drag and I said no but Nina took the cigarette and inhaled really deeply and then giggled, and Mr Roberts said that's *classy*, and I had to look away.) And in the art class he said this drawing is *classy*, and Nina purred some more, and I thought I was going to vomit. And then Mr Roberts's hand started hovering over my drawing. And I prayed he wouldn't say anything about it, but then his cheese and onion fingers touched the paper and left a greasy smudge on one side of my floating goat's skull, and he bent down and said to me in that low voice, but loud enough so everyone could hear: *you're trying too hard, don't try, just observe, relax*. And I held my breath so I didn't have to smell his, and I could feel my cheeks burn all the way through the rest of the class and into break. And later, when me and Nina were standing by the gates, Mr Roberts walked past with his rucksack over his shoulder, grinning to himself like a stupid schoolboy. And he said nice work, Nina, you're really coming along; I hope you'll be taking the Art 'O' Level. And she said yes, Michael, I will. And I looked at her because how did she know his first name? And Mr Roberts smiled and said good. And then he asked if we'd heard the latest Smiths album. And Nina said yes because we loved the Smiths and of course we had, although I was sure I loved the album more than she did because I was a vegetarian and knew about these things. And Mr Roberts said it was cool, Morrissey was cool, a *God*, he said. And Nina agreed. And then he said see you girls, stay out of trouble. And when he'd gone, I said I hated Mr Roberts. And Nina said he's sexy. And I said don't be disgusting. And Nina shrugged. And then the bell rang for the end of break and I pulled Nina's arm because we had to go to Biology and put things in Petri dishes, but she had that far-off look in her eyes I didn't like, the same look she'd had the night of Elvira's party, as if she knew something I didn't. And I shouted Nina! And she blinked and said, yeah, okay, coming.

It was the Saturday before Christmas and we were sitting on Nina's bed, doodling and listening to David Bowie – our favourite man in the whole world – well, Nina was doodling, I was just trying out my name in different signatures like I was famous while Nina drew figures of women with luscious curves. And then I looked up from the page and round at Nina's room, which was covered with Bowie posters and one of those prints of the lovers embracing called *The Kiss*. And that's when I noticed the two passport photos pinned to the wall. And I said who's that? And Nina didn't even look up before she said: my dad, and then her face went red. And I said what, because she'd never mentioned her dad before. And she said yeah, can't even get himself into the photo booth right, what a loser. And it was true: half his head was missing in both pictures so all you could see was the bottom of his face which made him look sad and old, his hair grey all over. And Nina said he's old, like she read my mind, too old for me to care about. And I thought why do you keep a picture of him on your wall then, but I didn't say anything because she was still red and I knew that wasn't like Nina at all. And when she wasn't looking I sneaked another peek at the pictures and I noticed there were creases on the prints, as if they'd been folded, and behind her dad's face there was this reddish glow, like a haze over the white backdrop. And Nina said can you stop looking at that please. And I stopped looking, but it didn't stop me thinking. And she said he's *pathetic*: he sends me tapes. And I said what kind of tapes. And she rolled her eyes and said you don't want to know, but I did. Play one, I said. And eventually she got up and fetched a shoe box from the shelf and tipped it onto the bed. And there were about fifteen tapes, all labelled in black ink: Music One, Two, etcetera. And she flipped one open and put it into the cassette player by her bed, and there was a hiss and a crackle and then the first note – a xylophone like we played at primary school – then a cymbal, then nothing. And she said I told you: it's pathetic; he calls it music. And I said what kind of music is that? And she said discordant, modern, I don't know. And then she ejected the tape and put Bowie back in. And we sang along to *Changes* as she shoved all the cassettes under the bed: *turn and face the strain, ch ch changes,* or at least I thought we were both singing but when I looked up I realised Nina wasn't singing at all: she had taken the photographs down from the wall and was very carefully, and perfectly, with a bright red pen, blotting out her dad's face.

The Bench Buddhay

Tariq Mehmood

Though a starched turban now covered Mangal
Singh's ageing hair, his tough roundish face was
clean shaven. Mangal Singh and his friends had
become a regular fixture on the Soho road, in
Handsworth. There were a number of benches up and
down the road, and all of them had their regulars. Many
secrets, old and young, past and present, were buried
in the minds of these old men. Sitting there for the
best part of the day, they patiently made mental notes
of who was driving around with who, which factories
had closed and where and how their children – and in
some cases their children's children – were wasting the
best years of their lives in forced idleness.

'You should not let a wife's doings so upset you,'
Allah Ditta said to Mangal Singh flippantly.

'It's not her doings that upset him, Allah Dittiya.
Whose wife doesn't do what a wife is not supposed to
do? And when a wife doesn't do what she's supposed to

do, doesn't mean that a man should do what he wasn't made to do?' said Qama Singh, who until then had sat quietly, gazing out at nothing in particular.

Mangal Singh lowered his head in shame.

'Qama Sian, I have never understood your philosophy,' Allah Ditta said. Turning to Mangal Singh he smirked and added, 'Yaar, lift up your head; things will get better. They always do...'

'It's not his head that's caused his problem,' Qama Singh interrupted Allah Ditta. 'It's not his head that won't stand up.'

'Your mouth and arse let out same things,' Mangal Singh protested.

'This is a matter of opinion, Mangal Sian,' Qama Singh chortled. 'What do you expect that poor woman to do?'

'She has now stopped cooking for me, and is even threatening to walk out on me as well,' Mangal Singh said, turning away from Qama Singh.

'She is a young woman and has to look at an old ass like you,' Qama Singh said. 'You know, Mangal Sian, I've got a solution for you.'

'What's that then?' Allah Ditta asked mischievously.

'There is this new medicine. It is supposed to do for a man what Mangal Sian needs to save his marriage.'

'Don't put him on wrong paths,' Allah Ditta said with a little guttural laugh. 'Didn't you hear about that old ghora who had a heart attack right in middle of doing his thing?'

'Noo!' Qama Singh laughed, coughing at the same time.

'But he was a *ghora*,' Mangal Singh said smiling broadly. '*He* didn't grow up drinking *lassi!*'

Someone among the Buddhay had lit a cigarette, which infuriated Qama Singh, who started to cough. He did this whenever he was angry.

'I've told you not to light up, especially in public,' Qama Singh protested as he spat on the floor between coughs. He brushed his beard with his right hand and with the other pushed Channan Ram, the smoker, as far away as his trembling arm would allow.

'Leave it be. You haven't got long to live anyway,' Mangal Singh chided Qama, to Channan Ram's relief.

'This is the first one for six months and look at you,' Channan Ram lied, 'and anyway, how can a cat go on Haj after eating a hundred mice?'

Qama Singh coughed. He understood Channan's inference and became embarrassed. He also coughed each time he was embarrassed. During his younger days he had had a passionate fling, and only Channan Ram knew who it was with, or at least that is what Qama Singh thought. The truth was that over the years the story of his love affair had been retold so many times that it had almost become a legend, and though a generation had now passed, she was still alive and it could still have dangerous implications

'Ohy, oh mundyo,' Allah Ditta interrupted the silence. His voice was filled with laddish excitement. 'Look at that girl's thighs,' he said, pointing towards a young woman with a flicker of his large, overgrown white eyebrows. The bench understood, and there was no sudden movement. Slowly, trying not to startle the prey, the Buddhay turned towards her, one by one, gently. Qama Singh even held his thinning beard. The young woman was lost in her own world. She was tall and pretty and wore a short skirt that at least covered her buttocks. Her long, long hair followed her in waves.

'Wah, wah, wah, youth,' Channan Ram said under his breath as he stubbed out his cigarette. He was the oldest and could hardly see beyond the end of his nose. Channan Ram suffered from the Alzheimer's disease and was forever getting lost. But he always found a way to get involved in whatever company he was in. Over the years he had forgotten just about everything at some time or other, and now had difficulty tying his shoe laces. Nevertheless, he was still a meticulously tidy man. He wore a loose turban which he tied himself. The twists and turns in the fold of the cloth were a piece of art that covered his head, giving his ageing body an elegant youthful appearance. Channan Ram understood his illness. He had developed a simple code. So long as he could tie his own turban in the way he wanted, he would be able to hold his life together. He had dismissed the suggestions of his family for him to wear a hat or else a pre-wrapped starched turban with simple logic: 'A man who does not have time to tie his own turban has no time for life.'

'Oh, Channaya, you're nothing but a blind old Hindu,' Allah Ditta retorted. The other Buddhay laughed. Qama Singh coughed. He always coughed when he laughed.

'I'll put a bacon sandwich with your corpse and bury you before I go up in smoke,' Channan Ram replied, nodding and smiling without looking at Allah Ditta.

'That's if you don't forgot,' said Allah Ditta under his breath, as he stole a glance towards the approaching young woman.

When she was a few yards from the bench, Channan Ram managed to see her outline. Though she was still out of earshot the bench went into precautionary silence.

'*Look* at those thighs.' Allah Ditta dropped a whisper into loaded silence. The girl was right in front of them. They could smell her excessive perfume.

'Just like her mother, Pago's,' Mangal Singh confessed. She had bounced passed them and was waiting for the traffic lights to change.

'Just like Pago's mother's as well,' Qama Singh added. The other old men turned towards him in astonishment.

Qama Singh coughed and spat on to the floor as every one wondered whether he was finally coming clean. But no sooner had the young woman disappeared then the conversation about her ended and the bench once again descended into a contemplative silence.

An articulated lorry, which had been slowly inching forward in a long line of traffic, came to a complete stop when it reached near the bench. The loud coughing of its untuned diesel engine all but drowned out the thoughts of the old men who were beginning to become irritated by the smell of the lorry's exhaust fumes. Mangal Singh stared impatiently at the traffic lights that were responsible for holding up the lorry. It seemed to him that the lights had stopped on red. He lowered his head and shut his eyes, but the red of the traffic lights hung in a dark void in his mind like a burning sun.

'Don't worry so much,' Qama Singh said softly to Mangal Singh. 'Time solves all problems.'

The red fireball flashed into oblivion as Mangal Singh lifted his head up and opened his eyes. The lorry was pulling itself through the traffic lights; thick black smoke gushed out of its rear.

'I know its all my fault – but there is nothing I can do,' Mangal Singh replied to Qama Singh sorrowfully.

'Whatever will happen will happen,' Qama Singh said, raising his voice in irritation. Pointing, with what remained of his index finger, at Mangal Singh, Qama Singh continued, 'We will see. But you are not a woman and you don't have to cry like one...'

'You always manage to bring women into every conversation,' Channan Ram interrupted. Before continuing he looked around. He felt something was missing but found it difficult to articulate his thoughts. The sight of the remains of Qama Singh's finger brought back a flood of memories. He began to relive the moments before the accident, which had led to Qama Singh's finger being amputated. Channan Ram looked at the scars of the fire on his own hand.

He had been in the yard of the foundry stacking ingots onto pallets that were then taken inside and thrown into a furnace by Qama Singh. That day it had rained and though Channan Ram had warned the foreman against rushing the job, his words had not been heeded. He was on his break and was walking past Qama Singh when the furnace had spat out molten aluminium. Had it not been for the fact that Channan Ram screamed a warning, Qama Singh would almost certainly have been killed. Qama Singh dived out of the way, but as he landed a large ingot fell onto his hand and crushed his index finger. As Channan Ram was pulling Qama to safety, the furnace spat out more boiling metal, parts of which had landed on his hand. He was lucky that his injuries were only skin deep.

'What have we not seen in our time, Mangal Sian?' Channan Ram said as images of the accident flashed through his mind. 'And we will help you get through this as well.'

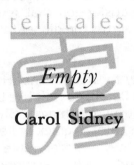

tell tales

Empty

Carol Sidney

A nd so it is always a curious sight he makes, walking down the car-logged street with Jewelle at his side. Mrs Doyle, his neighbour, watches him now as he makes steady progress along All Souls Avenue. Irish, inquisitive and birdlike, she is regularly perched by her bay window, musing about the odd couple who live across the road. Her only audience is her muzzled, elderly mother, who is permanently engaged to the television. But nothing Mrs. Doyle watches on TV can match the sight of a medium-built, middle-aged, quite nondescript white man making proprietorial gestures towards the black woman who often walks by his side. 'The size of her!' Mrs. Doyle has never seen anyone else go into their house, so perhaps, like his life, his house has a lot of space; it would need it, to hold a woman like that.

Mrs Doyle's curtain twitches. Derek Vane consciously thrusts his neck forward, somewhere between peacock and turkey. He loosens his hips, swinging them in rhythm to his shoulders, approaching his gate with a flourish, courteously allowing Jewelle to precede him. 'There you go,' he says to her, smoothing his greying, medium-brown hair. 'Give the old girls a treat,' he says to himself, and is rewarded by a violent shake of his neighbour's curtains. 'You've still got it, Derek, you dog!' He sighs with a satisfaction that is confirmed, hours later, as he gazes across the dinner table at his woman. His jewel.

Things are easy for Derek Vane. He has made them so. Affable, genial Derek, doesn't like to think too much. Thinking puts a strain on things. Gives them a sickly tinge that palls his spirit. A quick smile, likeable banter, an even temper; they are preferable to reality served raw and cold. And much has supported him in his fantasies thus far. A society still lingering in its colonial past. A group of friends, 'middle aged boozers' really, who won't pry too much, baffled enough by their own lives. Distant relations with his estranged father and his younger brother which have long since given way to a nonchalant shrug of his shoulders when he manages to think of them at all. No, if he thinks at all, it is about work. It does not give him as much pleasure these days, but it still provides some of the satisfaction he craves.

'I'm off down the *Lion*, love.'

Jewelle looks up from her plate.

'Will you be OK?' His attentiveness is calculating, smiling winningly at her with blue-grey eyes that sag at the sides to give him an adorable, sad, puppy-dog look.

Whether Jewelle loves him is difficult to tell. As much as she can, and just as impossibly, she blends into the background. At home, at work, on the street, her preoccupation, her obsession, is to become as small as possible. A tiresome trait she has acquired from she knows not where, it nevertheless dominates her every thought and action, providing an imperative which structures her day. She is grateful to him, of course, for the security he has given her. Financially she need not worry. But she is conscious that the things about her which repulse her, her size, her colour, are a draw for Derek. She is his prized possession, a trophy he takes private pleasure in, and after a lifetime of rejection, this is reason enough to stay.

'Go off. Have your fun,' she says, falling in with their Friday night routine of dinner, bath and bed for her; and dinner, a drink at *The Lion's Gate*, back home and then bed for him. Shifting heavily from her chair, she makes for the bathroom upstairs. He follows, and picks up his jacket. The contrast he makes to Jewelle is supreme. Where she towers, he is puny and indistinct. Her skin glistens a deep unfathomable brown, where his is a dullish grey. And her flesh, so much flesh. Sticky, sickly mounds of her flesh, gleaming and irrevocable, stacked up against his diminished frame, too rich, surely, for his paler constitution. But if Jewelle's flesh overwhelmed him, most often this is not an unpleasant sensation, and every day he marvels at the sight of her, this woman he has made his. Something is satisfied, a deep longing? An ache? A puzzle? Something had been stilled within him, because of her.

They meet at the bottom of the stairs and stand for an awkward minute until Derek moves forward and buries the moment in her flesh, his arms around her belly. Their differences make him seem more like her son than her partner.

'Thanks, love. You get an early night.' Grateful, he turns away.

Behind the closed front door, his eager footsteps sound down the path and Jewelle holds him in her mind's eye as he turns onto the pavement. She pauses. She is cautious. She waits, her head straining to the silence of the corridor. He has disturbed her before and she needs to be sure. A safe length and she begins her ritual behind the locked bathroom door. Cold tap. Running water. Towel on the floor to protect her knees. Two fingers touching the back of her throat. Her head slotted into the toilet bowl.

*

Sometime later Derek's key enters the lock and Jewelle tenses. These are the moments she dreads most, when that feeling of being overwhelmingly herself cannot be held in check. Emptied, she feels as right, as good, as normal, as deserving as she ever hopes to be. Maybe he'll just fall asleep on the couch downstairs.

'Jewelle!'

No. Not this time. The light uneven thud of his feet up the stairs is her cue to flinch. She buries her feelings somewhere under the flats of her feet, and arranges herself, despairing of the flesh that shifts so irrevocably. Mercifully, she knows it will be in the dark, and it will be a grope, a quick skirting of her flesh, a thrust into her body, and then a slumping end. Sometimes they are children and she, the bigger of the two, allows the smaller to play-ride her. Other times, the groping places the terrain of her flesh like a hammer at the centre of her forehead and another part of her heart dies. For Derek, conquering her belly and her buttocks is a sensation like no other. Like fucking a donkey or a horse, if his imagination could stretch that far. At his peak, he feels something restorative, the elation of dominating something that should be beyond his strength. And then he collapses in bliss.

*

But in the night, despite Derek's contented snores, something bubbles up and stirs within Jewelle. Maybe it was always there.

*

The haze after the night before never lasts long. As he rolls out of bed and slides in front of the bathroom mirror, Derek Vane notes the grey pallor of his skin, like a sign of death. Blacks are leaving the country, says the radio. Repatriating home. The Queen is going to make a speech about multiculturalism. A new golf club has recently opened and refused entry to a wealthy Cypriot man. Derek's eyes are more bloodshot than blue and he wonders if he said anything untoward last night, out with Jez and Phil. Jewelle's heavy tread squeezes her bulk around him and the outskirts of his mind grapples with something new, something he has been resisting. Is she bigger? Has she grown? Mentally he shakes himself. Of course not. She has always been a big woman. That's why he wants her.

A sudden 'boom!' goes off, somewhere near his right ear.

'Derek!'

A thud. Was it in his head? No, Jewelle has slipped on the wet floor and somehow lodged herself in the doorway.

'What are you doing, you stupid mare?' Derek wants to laugh. His usual banter, surely, will cover the moment.

'Help me! Derek, help me... I can't. I don't...'

'How d'yer do that?'

Derek Vane grips a leg and pulls. He is trying to be helpful.

'I can't...I – I...'

Derek catches her loose arm which is gesticulating despairingly. He stills it and pulls, and yet nothing shifts. Standing back, he jumps over her to try another angle.

'Derek, do something!' Jewelle's normal placid self approaches something like anger. But she is well and truly wedged, and all Derek can do is shake his head in disbelief.

*

Derek ventures downstairs, tentative. Somehow afraid. He has not been able to understand what has happened. He cannot deny something has. Through the slit of the open living room door, he spots Jewelle spread across their only couch. She is gazing at the TV, watching Saturday sport with excessive fascination, like an alien. He knows something must be said. The woman he has lived with for more than a year, with intimacy and care, his jewel, has melted away. In her place, this person, this thing, is not a woman anymore but a beast, a monster, a nightmare he may have conjured from the dark side of his own mind. He doubts he has the strength to tackle her. He doesn't know what she is. Doesn't know what *it* is. Still debating what to do next, she looks back suddenly and he catches his breath in fear.

Swallowing, he breaks the moment by striding into the room. He clears his throat and braves her beady eyes that are rapidly disappearing under the expanding folds of brown flesh.

'Jewelle, I've made a decision. You're not to go out anymore until you've got yourself under control.'

Jewelle blinks like a mute hog.

'You must realise...you'll draw attention to yourself. People will wonder what... well, whether...'

The hog stretches herself a little, seeking a more comfortable position, her flesh now spilling over the sides of what he always thought was a substantial couch. Derek clears his throat, trying once again for authority, but the terror in his voice is unmistakable.

'Y-you m-must know your p-place, Jewelle. I-I would've t-thought all w-women like y-you know that. Too much of y-you is.... well.... It w-won't do.'

Jewelle raises her hand to rub her nose and Derek shrieks in fear, stepping backwards into the little bay window. She is as placid as ever, even kind. She has always deferred to him.

'Of course, Derek. Whatever you say. I will get smaller. I know I will.'

But, as if to defy her words, both Jewelle and Derek pause to watch her body expand some more. Jewelle is now, literally, everywhere. Soon she will not be able to move at all. Soon her stomach sits in the living room while her shoulders have pushed beyond the ceiling. Soon her legs will extend beyond the outer walls with poor, poor Derek gasping what air and oxygen he can, pressed up against the window, unable to move, unable to speak. Like the line drawing of a dead man.

*

And so it is, one day, not long after that fateful Saturday morning, that Mrs Doyle looks out of her beloved bay window. In an instant she is scurrying to the phone, running past her baffled mother. She dials and begins to speak, suddenly unsure whether she is

requesting the fire brigade, an ambulance or the police.
To be sure, she asks for all three.

tell tales

Belladonna

Romesh Gunesekera

Senhor da Silva spotted me before I could nip out of the way. Good Morning, he said, and glanced into my basket.

Molasses today, hmm? Flour and nuts? Baking another of your delightful cakes? He sniggered as though he knew more than he should.

I told him I was making a cake for the Captain. The sun was shining bright and clean and I had nothing to hide.

Very good, he said with a big smirk. It is the Captain's birthday on Saturday, of course. And Senhora Dona Luisa, if you're making a cake, there must be a celebration.

I could hardly say no.

Senhor da Silva waggled his head knowingly. At your house?

I nodded. Four o'clock on Saturday.

Excellent. Gonçalves can play the guitar.

*

Pedro was the one who wanted to give the Captain a cake.

He straightened himself out and said, I feel indebted, you know, after the Captain brought that oil to fix my back. And I think he could do with a buck up.

My husband is an educated man and very knowledgeable about breeding fruit and veg, but bucking up, I can tell you, is not his thing. For months I've been doing my own experiments, taking a leaf out of his book. I have tried every kind of buck up on Pedro – roasted beans, dried green beetles, crushed amaryllis – but to no avail. All he ever felt was backache. It is not that I want to be wanton; it is just that time is running out.

I blame my father.

I'll find you a handsome fellow with the face of Adonis and the back of a bull, he promised. Then in that awful summer of 1657, when the gales ravaged our poor Madeira, he got tangled up in someone's rig and fell in the harbour. I had thought he was indestructible, but he drowned. His precious list of the eligible was washed out into the middle of the Atlantic. Ill luck hung around our house like a bad smell and no one came near for ages. No one except for Pedro.

*

I told Pedro about the birthday party on Saturday. Oh good, he said. My banana is in flower and Senhor da Silva will be very impressed.

Why do you want to impress that man?

He has the money, you see, my dear. Pedro wagged his skinny little finger. And I think he might be interested in a little proposition I have.

This is what Mama should have warned me about. The day men start proposing to other men while they have perfectly good wives of their own twiddling their thumbs at home.

Mark my words, Pedro said. With my banana and my bean, Madeira will become the number one plantation again. You can forget America and all that wretched sugar business.

Fine. I said. Go preen your bananas for da Silva. I have a cake to make.

*

The basic recipe I use is Mama's. She learnt it from her mother. Grandma had made the strangest, darkest, moistest cake for Mama's wedding. She claimed it took her nine months, but it was probably nine hours plus a thimbleful of brandy every month while she waited for the day to be fixed.

The original recipe belonged to a baker's son from Devon who had jumped ship in Funchal at the turn of the century. As a young girl, Grandma had fallen for his strange accent and peculiar taste in puddings. But then, one day, before anything could happen, he left for the New World. Mama said the wedding cake was actually his English Christmas pudding that Grandma had tried to replicate in a fit of reminiscence.

Mama said the cake worked wonders for her marriage and therefore made it every anniversary as a kind of fillip. She cut out the eggs from the original recipe, and the nine months of brooding, and made other modifications each year until, by the time I got hold of it, the cake was unique. Grandma's mountain of flour and fat and sugar had settled into a round as flat as a cow-pat and about the same in colour, but it tasted like honey and smelt of heaven. Any man but my Pedro would be in rapture at the mere whiff of it.

For the Captain, I thought I might add a little nutmeg to see what would happen. But first I had to warm the pig fat with the molasses, then join the flour with the sugar and sink the fermented dough. As I threw in the handfuls of raisins and candied peel and almonds, I thought of how the Captain had come to the house the day Pedro's back had seized up. The Captain was a strong man and had no trouble carrying the bath into the garden. He spoke stirringly about the restorative powers of oil and water warmed by the sun. He had travelled very far in the world. All the way to the cinnamon island and the home of the clove. But would he like cake? I put the wine in and the spices, and lastly a few scrapings of nutmeg and hoped for the best.

In the morning a yellow bird came to my window, twittering like a drunk. Pedro was already up and out in the garden in his sandals. He likes to start the day squatting by the fig tree and contemplating the hills. I don't know what he is up to lolling on his haunches like that. It can't be good for a man's spine. One time I asked him: Hey, what's going on? Is it your stomach? Too much red wine? But he wrinkled up his nose and wouldn't answer. It's not that he is deep; he just does not know how to speak.

*

By Saturday the rich, syrupy smell of the mixture clung to everything in the house.

Pedro, you like it? I tried to catch him before he scuttled out. Pedro?

Sometimes he acts as if I don't even exist. Nobody else I know does that, so why does the man who is my husband want to do that?

What about lunch, then? I asked. You expect me to make lunch?

Nothing for me. Just the cake for the Captain.

He says that, but the next thing I know he'll be at the sausage or the pork fat, nibbling bits and pieces as if to show the whole world what a useless cook I am except for mud pies and flat black cake. It is just not right and I'm not having it.

Get the fire going then, I told him. That at least he can do: light a fire in a fireplace if not in the heart of a real woman. Meanwhile I put the cake mixture into my mother's baking pot and prepared everything else. It is not a difficult business. You just need a dish that closes properly.

*

I heard the guitar before I saw them coming up the lane. Gonçalves and da Silva were laughing.

I blinked back the belladonna – Mama's best eye brightener — and went out.

The Captain was lagging behind. Senhor da Silva stopped and waited for him to catch up.

This way. Pedro guided them to the terrace where I had put out the chairs and the table. Captain, he said, this was father-in-law's chair. The best for you because ... he paused and waved his hands as though he was a priest getting a congregation to follow him. Because it is your birthday. We all clapped our hands. Gonzo struck a chord and made a kind of strangled sound that may have been poetry once, long ago, before the likes of that Lourenço de Almeida and Vasco da Gama had even seen the sea. He plucked a few more strings and launched into the deadly lilt of a ship in trouble.

The Captain cleared his throat and looked grimly at the guitar.

Senhor da Silva produced his bottle of wine and had the audacity to wink at me. It was a good thing he hadn't poured it out and handed the glasses around because if I had one in my hand I would have flung it in his face.

I swallowed my anger and pulled out the cake. Captain, I said. This is for you.

For me? Despite the fifty years he'd borne on sea and land fighting potentates and Hollanders, tigers and sharks, feasting in the east and the west, when he dipped his finger in my cake and licked it, he looked delighted.

Pedro saw that Senhor da Silva had noticed the purple banana flower and took him to it. Gonzo drooled at the dark, juicy mass of cake and got a bit more baila into his song.

The Captain stuck his fingers in again.

So, how is it? I asked this paragon who had seen the whole world and now had come to me to tuck into a cake of honey.

Oh my, he murmured. Cinnamon, cardamom, nutmeg. Senhora Dona Luisa, this is simply... scandalous.

The Princess and the Pea

Gemma Weekes

You've taken to wearing your princess dresses everyday, with ringlets and a tiara and even the glass slippers, which aren't very comfortable. You wear the damsel gear even in Upper Clapton on a weekday. Even when you're waiting for a bus or doing your laundry. Even now, in the midst of a winter storm. The rain is distorting your make-up, putting a riot into your curls. You're dragging those silken hemlines through the mud and cigarette butts like a deranged Miss World contestant.

You are a freezing cold, super-hot mama. A princess lost. Tired. Hungry. (Not that you eat, of course. Nothing but the tiniest slivers of wild pheasant, a sweet meat, the odd poison apple. Kebabs? Of course not!) You're fed up and you're starting to lose it.

A real princess is born to be rescued! Everybody knows this. It's the whole fucking point. *Everybody*

89

know this. But there's not another bonafide royal in sight, only lager lads and old pervs. You try not to mumble these words aloud as you walk down the filthy streets. Even the crackheads and crazies know to seek shelter in weather like this. In fact, they're smirking at you right now from corner shop doorways.

'Hey Princess Ghetto!' they yell and laugh from their shadows.

'Piss off!' you reply, the words bounce so strange and ugly out of that cushiony little mouth. 'Peasants!' But you're vex and you're not afraid to show it. Flaming cheeks, lowered brow, wet hair. You're pretty messed up. You step hard on the pavement, despite your exhaustion. Head up, shoulders back. *Click clack, click clack,* each step like a gunshot. Floating ain't easy after a few miles.

It's not too much to ask, is it? For a real princess? To be rescued? Look at those bones! You're a real china doll, a real glass angel – even in the fluorescent street lights.

And nobody told you that getting rescued would be such bloody hard work. Maybe because there aren't too many evil stepmothers, warlocks or witches, trolls or goblins these days with the time or inclination to work on a collaborative project of such magnitude. Mostly these days they drive buses or dispense parking tickets, even run countries.

And fragility is a very important quality for a real princess to display, but it's very difficult to cultivate successfully in a shit-hole like London. By now you've been the subject of several botched rescue attempts, and you've had to develop some smarts just to make it from one idiot prince to the next. See, it's very important that you survive. You can't actually die or anything – if you do, there won't be any wedding. As you well know, there has to be a wedding. Without the wedding, your story isn't one that anybody wants to hear.

'Excuse me...'

You're catapulted eight foot in the air by shock. (Well, not literally, of course – real princesses are the perfect incarnation of grace and poise; you merely raised one of your naturally gorgeous eyebrows.)

'Excuse me, miss!' It's a little man in uniform; he's lightly grabbed you by the arm and is trying very hard not to look through your soaking dress. 'Are you a real princess?'

'Yes,' you say. 'Yes I am. The genuine article.'

Finally, somebody who understands you! The mingled relief and anticipation is intense, drumming a little calypso in your chest cavity. It's a palace! A sudden palace, smacked right in the middle of the high street. It's red, gold and glitzy – a huge version of one of those really over-the-top Chinese restaurants. The little guardsman bows deeply and motions at his colleagues to open the gates.

You've never seen a palace around here before, but you, of all people, should be used to a bit of magic now and then.

You're lead up the drive, past luxury cars and hedges trimmed in the shape of animals. To look too happy or shocked, of course, would be unseemly, so you maintain a calm and serene visage.

Breathe.

At the front door he stops and bows again. You're shivering now and completely consumed by the idea of being warm. You can't wait. The windows look amber-hot, toasty as an armpit. If you had an axe, you'd hack your way through the front door! But then there are footsteps.

The door is flung open. 'Dear heavens!' And there stands a chubby, middle-aged woman. 'I do believe you're a real princess! Come in before you catch your death of cold, you poor thing.'

You walk over the flagstones and are taken to a reception room dominated by a big, burning fireplace. The lady that you assume to be a housekeeper brings you a heavy blanket and tells you to relax while she tells the queen about you.

And it's so good under that lovely warm blanket in front of that lovely warm fire. You snuggle up and stare into the flames - maybe this is it! Where there's a queen, a prince can't be far off. Maybe he'll be better than the others.

The last almost-rescue occurred when some prince from South London tried to rescue you from the tower of an evil landlord. He ended up falling five stories and breaking his back. After you took the lift down to the ground floor and called for an ambulance, you experienced the first sharp piercing of doubt. This might never happen. You took out your pocket mirror and noticed that your nose was getting decidedly less button-like. Your mouth was getting an urban twist to the corners. You were even beginning to grow little biceps in your thin arms from all the exertion of being a distressed damsel.

But now, you have a feeling that everything's going to be fine.

'Excuse me, your highness,' says the housekeeper as she re-enters the room. 'The queen asked me to run some tests.'

She sits next to you on the big sofa and whips out a little tape measure. With it, she measures the distance between your eyes, the distance between your nose and hairline, between your mouth and nose, between your chin and your hairline. She asks you to stand up in your wet clothes and strip. You feel faintly humiliated, but do as she asks. She measures your breasts, your waist, your thighs. Even the circumference of your neck and head. Then she does your hands and feet.

'Right!' She exclaims happily. 'Seems like you check out, love. You really must be a genuine princess.'

She then gives you a robe to put on and asks you to recite a poem and sing some opera. You do so. By now you're quite excited. After all, this prince must be of an awesome calibre to demand all of these tests.

After you've finished singing, she takes you to the kitchen and asks you to bake a cake from scratch. You do so. You are exhausted. You don't take a bite of your own gorgeous, fluffy cake. You know she's watching you.

'Lovely,' she says. 'I'll take you up to meet the Queen now.'

And you both go down some corridors and up some steps and through some doors until you end up in a huge, high-ceilinged bedroom.

'Um, where's the queen?' you enquire timidly.

'Good heavens,' laughs the housekeeper you're beginning to hate. 'You can't meet her in this state!'

And off you go into the bath. And you're given a dress to wear, and the maids brush, buff, pluck and polish you until you're glossy as a fashion mag. And you're so tired by now that you're verging on delirium. Plus, you still haven't eaten.

'Now you're ready to dine with the queen,' says Housekeeper Bitch Lady.

Dine, you think. Food!

You're taken to the queen's personal dining room where she's seated at the head of the table. 'Good evening,' she says, regal in a dark velvet gown. She smiles opaquely, a creamy glint in her eye. 'I'm so happy to meet you.'

'Likewise, your majesty.' You curtsy all the way to the floor, like you've learned.

'Oh do get up, dear,' says the queen. 'What a lovely little thing you are. Won't you have some supper with me?'

The table is loaded with food and wine; the smell alone is enough to make you swoon with hunger. But you're no idiot. You place seven peas and a chicken leg on your plate. And then you comment on how stuffed you are when you've eaten it.

She asks you, finally, what your name is and what led you to be walking around in a freezing storm. Your name is Princess. Yeah, and you've heard the Princess Princess joke a thousand times. It's not funny anymore. And it's very odd, but it's not until this moment that you actually remember who you are. It feels like you've been out in the world forever, waiting to be rescued.

'Well,' you begin, 'my parents are the King and Queen of Chatsworth. When I was very young, my father went away and we never heard from him again. My mother was so distraught she went quite mad. In fear for my life I fled the palace, hoping to find my father... I searched the land.' At this point, you look up under your lashes for emphasis. 'I hoped, one day, that he would be able to give me away in marriage. But since I left, I have heard nothing of my father. Instead, I've been plagued by horrible weather and evil forces, all of which have lead me here. To you.'

Demurely, the queen dashes a single tear from her eye. 'Oh, how awful!' she says. At this moment, you notice that the queen's face is actually quite weird. It's stretched a little too tightly over her skull, and the lips are close to exploding with fake ripeness. *Oh dear*, you think gleefully.

'You *must* stay the night,' she says, throwing her fork down. 'I've searched everywhere for a real princess. In the morning, you'll meet my son! Prince Desmond.'

Yes! Yes! Yes! 'That would be lovely.' You show her nothing but polite interest, though inside you're going off like fireworks. Real princesses always maintain an air of serenity. Yes! Yes! Yes!

'Mathilda!' she yells gracefully, and the housekeeper arrives. 'Please prepare a suite for Princess Princess.' To her credit, she doesn't emit so much as a chuckle.

When you're shown to your room you don't know what the hell it is you're looking at. The room is big and sumptuous, but the bed is a joke. There are twenty mattresses layered one on top of the other, and twenty duvets laid on top of that. It's piled so high there's barely any room between the bed and the ceiling.

'We want you to be extra comfortable,' says Mathilda.

In the morning, after a couple of butlers have helped you down from the bed, you realise that your body is covered in bruises. You can't figure it out; the bed was soft as marshmallows.

At breakfast, the queen eyes your bruises. 'Did you sleep well, my dear?'

'Oh no,' you say, in your little princess voice. 'I slept *awfully*. My body is covered in bruises!'

The queen smiles for a moment, and then bursts out, 'It was me! It was me! I ordered Mathilda to place a single pea under all of the mattresses. I thought that if you were sensitive enough to feel it, you'd have to be a real princess!'

And now you're truly baffled, because you know the queen is nuts to think that anyone could feel a single pea through twenty mattresses. But here you are! Black and blue.

You laugh prettily, though your thoughts are vicious. 'Oh, what a prank! Well here you see it. I'm a real princess, real as diamonds.' And you're thinking, 'You're a real queen. Did the surgery hurt?' But then she's speaking again.

'Do you want to meet Prince Desmond? Now that we've found a Real Princess, you should get married right away!'

'I'd love to!' you reply, still pondering on the origin of your bruises.

'Well...' says the queen, 'he's in the...' Her speech descends into an incoherent mumble.

'Excuse me?' you say humbly. 'Could you repeat that?'

'He's in the games room playing Playstation. Burning incense.'

'Oh.'

When you get to the games room, the prince is waiting. He's tall but grungy looking. He hasn't shaved, but his bones are perfect under the ill-fitting clothes and un-groomed hair.

'Hello.' He says. A soccer game is paused on the big screen telly behind him. You smell something and it's not incense, lets put it that way. It's green and comes in little bags.

Suddenly, you notice that he has a baseball bat balanced under one of his hands.

Bruises. Baseball bat. Bruises. Baseball bat.

'My mum's one crazy bitch.' He smiles. 'You don't know how many girls have come through here. I saw you from the window last night,' he says, taking a toke on his 'incense'. 'I love you. You're one sexy ting, man. I want to keep you.'

Some rescue.

Right, you think, chucking your tiara in a corner of the room. There's no way you're going back out in this weather.

For Zahid Mubarek

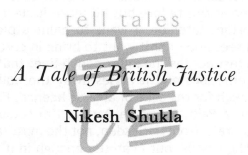

tell tales

A Tale of British Justice

Nikesh Shukla

They say that, creatively speaking, the edge of chaos is the best place to be. At the moment, I live my entire life on the edge of chaos. And I don't feel creative. I feel afraid. Afraid because sometimes chaos crosses that line.

Anyways, enough with metaphors and conceits. I've been here six months. Locked up. Banged up. Fitted up. All terms ending in 'up'. False hope, I say. Six months. And before you hear me protest my innocence, let me just get on with it, face up to it and say, yeah, I did it. Yeah, it was me, you got the right man, copper. I did it. I stole a pack of double A batteries. Here I am. Banged up for nicking a three squids fifty pack of batteries. My first offence too. That's the killer. They've got me fearing for my safety and my sanity in Britain's worst Young Offender's Institute for a first offence of petty shoplifting. A whiter defendant would have gotten away with a fine, I reckon. Other kids are in here for heavy drugs or raping their teachers or beating rival gangs up or manslaughter. One kid robbed an off-licence with a gun. And then there's me. Reggie fucking Kray.

This YOI is notorious for it's goings on. We've heard about the kids being beaten, guards looking the other way whilst cliques rule, staff-encouraged racial gladiatorial contests, violence, drugs, rape, it's all here.

I hinted at this before but I'll make it clear because it's important later on. I want to paint a picture for you, you see, and I don't want to bring in certain facts until the last act, as the killer punch line: that's unfair on your emotions and it pisses away the bullshit I've gone through for the sake of artistic licence. Fuck that. I'm Asian, a Paki, a Wog, a Darkie, I'm coloured. I'm Hindu Gujarati, from Harlesden, not the most salubrious neck of the woods, but I can see enough in it to call it home. So yes, me Asian, I Asian. Dark, ethnic, you know how it goes.

Last week they turned down my request to move cells. Again. I keep telling them I am really scared of my cellmate. I've been bunked down with him for six months and the dude gives me the creeps. I've written home loads to mum and my bro telling them about him and how he puts the fear of God in me. They assure me they've been hassling the guvnor to move me because I might not be safe. It's okay now though. One more night and I'm out of here. One more night, one more kip and I am gone into the morning light. I can't wait to walk outside, breath in the fresh air of the free, see my mum and my bro and hug them and just drive away and never come back. I find it hard to feel much regret for what I did. It was such a small offence, like nicking a cola bottle from the penny sweets section. I'm hardly a danger to society. I will now be going the extra mile in keeping my nose clean when I get out however.

I keep my nose clean in here. I know that some kids are here for far more serious crimes than me and it wouldn't take much for an incident to spark. I don't really have any friends. I don't say much to anyone. I read, I shit, I sleep, I eat, I fast, I pray, I watch and I wait. Each day takes me closer to being out and back in the comfort of my family again. I don't want to make it faster or slower. I certainly don't want to get into any trouble. I want to be a ghost and haunt the corridors, teaching myself the self-discipline of waiting. Praying, daydreaming and waiting constitute large parts of my day. In the repetitive cycle of our daily routine, these are the only times I can block out all around me.

Last night, 'Romper Stomper' was on the telly. All the boys crowded round to watch it, a violent film with Russell Crowe as a neo-Nazi thug attacking Vietnamese. The violence is unflinching and, as calculated acts of racism, completely debilitating to watch. I walked away, choosing to bask in my own solitude as the cold draughty winter's night crept over us. My last night, and all I wanted was quiet. I sat in my room, making mental sketches of paintings I'm yet to draw and doodles I'm yet to make. Peter stayed, watching the film. He devoured every frame, cheering on the violence, egging on the hatred. He got caught up on the lingering adrenaline and banged his feet on the table and floor, filling the empty hum of the halls and the flickering lights with his foot-stomps.

Peter's my cellmate.

Nice bloke really. Well, if you take nice to mean the devil incarnate. It's not that he has anger management issues; it's that he doesn't manage his anger at all. It's not that his tattoos are covered in racist soundbites and images; it's that he uses these as a code for living.

The bitter contempt and empty vacant stare in his eyes display a million boots stamped into black stomachs and brown backs, a thousand and one knives in a thousand and one sides, echoes of the smacks of punches laid on minorities, kicks clattering in the hollowness of his mind, screams. He has KKK tattooed on his forehead. He has British bulldogs and Combat 18 on his forearms. His back... well, it accurately depicts rivers of blood.

The first time I saw I was being locked down with him, it chilled me to my bone. Everyone knows him: he has a rep. He is a British bulldog. The blacks and browns don't touch him, don't go near him. I thought them putting me in a cell with him was some kind of sick joke, some trial by fire, some twisted initiation ceremony for me. I rode it out for my first night, but his whispering got to me. All night, he was awake, whispering, Paki this and darkie that...I would start to doze off and he would immediately spring off the metal-framed bunk-bed and start pacing the cell, the stomping arrhythmic pacing of his bare feet crushing into the cold floor.

I'd stay awake, listening to his hoarse but quiet mutterings. Often, in the middle of the night, it would get too much for him and he would turn the desk lamp on and write a letter to his brother, reading the letter out to himself as he went, writing down his filthy racist rhetoric, recording his dark thoughts and sleepless rants for posterity. He'd talk about me and what he would do to me, given the chance, about how I was filth and needed exterminating. He would write in just his boxer shorts, and those rivers of blood would flow towards me in my half-asleep daze. Each word would shake me, sending gunshots through my torso, ripping me in half. Hate-filled, murderous dark words with no redemption.

I would ask to be moved. I would tell the guards that I feared for my safety and that Peter was a racist who just needed an excuse to throttle me to death. The guards would tell me to keep my nose clean and get on with my time and he would probably leave me alone. I told them about the letters and how he wrote down fantasies about murdering me and how murdering me could trigger off the race war he'd always dreamed of. The guards would look at me like I was one of those paranoid conspiracy theory nuts. I tried to make appointments with the guvnor to tell him, but I never got given the chance to talk to him. I wrote letters home and my mum and my brother wrote letters back and letters to the government and still, I was left with...

'And the Paki on lockdown with me. He'll be the first. Fucking curry arse, stinking up my cell with his stench. I'll get him, don't you worry bro. He ain't leaving here walking, I'm telling you that. Sometimes I get so hyped-up inside myself, I feel like I could, you know. Sometimes I feel like he won't even leave here breathing. That's my mind state. Rivers of blood, white right... your loving brother, Peter.'

Last night 'Romper Stomper' was on the telly. Peter stayed up to watch it. Last night, I was sat in my room, drawing in my mind, trying to make some sort of sense out of the last six months. In here for the flimsiest of charges, well, they need cells full, how else they gonna get private investors without bums on seats. Thrown in with a racist, made to watch the sickening purposeful divide created between blacks and whites, made to take part in a mini-race war that's for larks and small childish bets between the guards. I win and you're on slop duty etc. It's nearly all over though. The dawn's rising.

I feel so tired. The last six months have been a painful stasis for me and it's nearly all over. I feel tired. Peter is clomping down the corridor just as my eyes are closing for a final time, my final sleep on the block. Tomorrow's a mile away. And I drift off....

I don't hear Peter's feet stamping, his heart thumping with insane adrenaline. I don't hear him look at me and my packed bag and call me a filthy Paki. I'm so tired I don't even hear him rip up his white sheet and place it on his head, like a Grand fucking Wizard. It's ridiculous how I definitely don't hear the table crash onto its side and his sheer brute strength rip a table leg clean off. The last thing I hear, which startles me awake, is the crunch of the table leg crashing down on my nose and sending it upwards into my brain, snapping the front of my skull and killing me almost instantly. Peter continues to bash me all over but I've lost the will and energy to fight. He screams at me, 'Darkie come here, Darkie won't leave,' over and over. Inside I'm just a scared little boy, ready to go home. Three pound fifty nick, six months living with a violent racist. A death that begins with my nose being broken, ends with me slumped on the floor having been pulled off the bed, the table leg embedded in my gluteus maximus.

No one listened. No one was there. No one cared. No one was looking out for me, or out for him. Rehabilitation wasn't even an issue. A waste of a life. If only my legacy wasn't kept in legal courts whilst judges decide over the simplest of facts. Why? No one knows, even those who should can't give my mother and my brother a straight answer. I don't blame Peter. He shouldn't have been there. He needed mental care. I don't blame myself. I shouldn't have been there. And when you absolve both of us of real blame, when you're looking at the causes... all you're left with is British Justice. Just us.

This story is dedicated to my mother, who loved to swim, and used to dream about swimming. She was getting up to swim at six in the morning until four weeks before she died, too young. I hope she was finally freed into water.

tell tales

Blue

Maggie Gee

The woman had lived through the longest day, which was boiling hot, in the city, pressing and sieving her into tiny pieces. She had five children; they all needed something, though the elder ones were at university.

'Mum!'

'Mum!'

'Mum!'

'Mum!'

'MU-U-M!!'

'Sorry,' she said. 'Sorry.'

She worked in a dry cleaner's, cleaning other people's clothes. That day, two of the machines had broken down. She had lost three ties and an expensive jacket. A woman came in and said she was a thief. A man had called her an idiot.

'Sorry,' she said. 'Sorry, sir.'

The air was dry and chemical. She wished she could wash the clothes in the river. She and her mother used to do that together.

At three, the woman cleared up to go home. Cleaning other people's clothes made her dirty; she itched from the solvents; she smelled of sweat. She pulled a white hair from her dark cotton shirt. Now she must go home and cook for her husband.

The traffic was a solid wall of metal. In her own metal box it got hotter and hotter. She hung one arm outside the open window. Then she saw a man in the car alongside, making obscene gestures and grinning at her. She drew in her arm and closed the window, but she heard him yell, 'Bloody women drivers!'

'Sorry,' she muttered, feeling small and frightened.

Then something inside her began to expand. Something like a distant pool of blue water. She heard the traffic horns, the revving engines, the man who thought she was a bloody woman, but inside her head there was a great pool of quiet. She drove off the road and abandoned her car.

She began to walk down the familiar track. All her life she had been too busy. She hadn't come here since she was a girl, but her feet remembered the way to go.

A beggar sat by a baking wall. 'Give me money, rich woman,' he said, reproachfully.

The woman had worked all day for almost nothing. 'No,' she said. 'No, sorry.'

She kept on walking as he shouted after her. A cloud of blue butterflies drifted towards her across the dry fields, and danced alongside her, so she could no longer see his small, cross shape.

A little further on, by a small ruined temple, a gang of teenagers were howling with laughter. They had painted slogans on the walls. 'Have you got the time, old woman?' they shouted. 'Tell us the time!' They pulled at her wrist. They didn't want the time, they wanted to hurt her.

'No,' she said. 'No, sorry.' A butterfly was spread where her watch had once been.

Now the track led on past the elaborate back gardens of the large new houses that faced the sea. People had erected gates and fences where she had once wandered with a troupe of goats. A uniformed man with a revolver suddenly stepped out from behind a hedge.

'What are you doing here?' he asked. His dark glasses bored into the hole in her sleeve, scraped up and down the dust on her legs. 'We don't want beggars here, woman. Get back where you belong, pauper.'

'No,' she said, 'No, sorry,' and the cloud of butterflies bobbed up around his head, making him shudder and flap his arms, unable to speak, unable to fly, while she slipped past him, on down the path.

A little further on, two workmen were lounging in the shade of the fence, eating oranges. One licked his fingers elaborately, and grinned at her, his big teeth shining. She saw that they were not from these parts.

'Do you want an orange, my beauty?' he said. 'Come and sit down in the shade with us.'

She hunched her shoulders and hurried past them.

'What, so pretty and so proud?' he asked her, letting his eyes travel over her body. 'Why can't you talk to a fellow human being?'

'No, sorry,' she said to them, her eyes on the ground, feeling guilty and naked.

Then the other man started to jeer at her: 'In any case, you're an ugly old bag, and...'

Before he could finish, the butterflies landed all over his lips, on the tip of his tongue, and he stopped, and spluttered, and the woman walked on.

A tiny snicket led off to the right past a sweet-scented patch of reseda blossoms. She remembered, with a pang, her mother's grave. Her mother lay waiting in the little cemetery, pleading for something that life had not given her. Her thirsty voice whispered, 'Please, daughter.' But how could she make things right for her mother? How could she ever bring enough flowers?

The cemetery lay in the wrong direction.

'No,' she said. 'Sorry, dear one.'

She picked a tiny spire of sweet reseda, and the hot wind carried it towards her mother.

The last part of the track was beyond the arch of the new white university. She was proud that her elder children went there. An ancient scholar sat bowed to the ground, reading a heavy tome, in the shade of the arch. He wrinkled up his eyes at her, over gold glasses.

'Where are you going, young woman?' he asked. 'This place is only for those who love learning.'

'My children love learning,' the woman replied.

'Where are your books?' he insisted, sharply. 'None of the unlearned come through here. Go back home and study, young woman.'

'No,' she said. 'No, sorry,' and two of the butterflies flew from her shoulders and landed, one each, on his spectacle lenses, so he could no longer peer at her.

In the distance, under a spreading tree, her elder children were debating with others. Usually they only saw her in the kitchen. They spotted her just as she was leaving the campus and heading on down towards the wide white sand.

'Mum,' they called, astonished. 'Mum! MU-UM! Where are you going?'

Her heart tugged and pulled, but the core of her was deep blue certainty, an ocean of water.

'Nowhere,' she whispered. 'Sorry, children,' and the butterflies swarmed into a flickering, glistening veil of blue air that hid her from sight. She was alone; all the voices faded.

She padded across the blazing sand. Glad, glad: everything was glad. She knew she could only bear it for a few seconds, but a few seconds would be enough. She took off her clothes. In the distance, people shouted. But the butterflies covered every inch of her body, floating up like blue steam as she slipped into the water. Cool, edgeless, it became her skin. A blue cloud hung on the blue sea wind. She was invisible. She was her soul. Mysterious, liquid, endless, whole.

Breathe our Confidence

Rachel Trezise

It all began on Victoria's thirtieth birthday. She was sitting at the breakfast table in the conservatory, her towelling bathrobe tea-stained and protruding over her premenstrual potbelly. A young woman yesterday, but only a woman today. November was a stupid time to be born because people were too concerned about Christmas to bother caring. Jesus was far more important than Victoria, so now tinsel eclipsed everything autumnal, including her having been alive for three decades.

She stared morosely through the UPVC window frame at the foliage in the back garden. The conservatory that she'd lusted after for months before Stephen bought it looked depreciated and ridiculous, like a silly plastic Wendy House a kid cries for only to grow out of it a year later. In the brochures it looked like a necessity for a happy life. Now it was twelve panes of glass to wash with vinegar and wipe with washing up liquid every weekend - to keep it looking virginal – as though nobody had ever looked through it. But what Victoria saw when she strained past the ginger rivulet marks was a horse chestnut belly-flop out of the old tree, bounce hard on the crazy paving, and crack like an egg yolk out of its prickly shell. Victoria stood up to see the conker, newborn and shining against the grey of the concrete patio. It had popped out of itself, just like she had. Who was to say maturity wasn't as valuable as youth? Now she was a butterfly.

Stephen came from the kitchen in his boxer shorts and shirt. He was carrying a platter high in the air with one hand and a jug of fruit juice in the other. 'Bucks fizz,' he said, leaning and lowering the silver tray onto the table cloth, 'and this, your birthday present.' What he put down in front of her was a cake shaped crudely into a pair of comedy breasts. The red icing in the centre of either sphere poked up like steeples to mimic erect nipples. It was the kind of uncouth idea that women like her sister, who regularly attended *Ann Summers* parties, came up with for their common law husbands while they sucked pineapple flavoured alcopop out of penis-shaped drinking straws.

'Don't look so offended,' Stephen said. 'What is it? Think about it.'

'It's a cake shaped like a pair of tits,' Victoria said.

'It's a cake shaped like a big pair of tits,' Stephen said, smiling. 'I'm going to pay for your breast enlargement!'

'What breast enlargement?' Victoria said. 'I've never said anything about a breast enlargement.' And she hadn't; not since Carys Goodwin called her 'fried egg titties', in Form Four Maths class. 'At least I can get a boob job,' had been her retort. 'You'd need a forklift to fix your fat face.'

114

'C'mon Vick,' Stephen said. 'You're always on about them.' He nodded at the undefined ruffles around the torso of her tatty robe. 'I've booked the appointment. Look!'

Victoria flicked through the information pack. It came wrapped in cellophane and pink ribbon like the once in a lifetime gifts you bought in chemists and newsagents on the high street. The receptionist at work got a helicopter flying lesson on Mother's Day. Victoria had thought that was absurd. What could her receptionist do with *one* flying lesson? But suddenly it seemed like quite a nice idea, better than a week in a clinic where a surgeon proposed to slice her chest open and force feed it silicone until it filled a double D cup.

She closed the pamphlet and tried to lift her downcast face into something like a grin. She'd been trained from birth to look grateful for the shitty gifts her relatives spared whilst saving up for Christmas time, the real deal. 'Breathe Our Confidence,' the words on the cover read above a soft focus photograph of a woman, probably Victoria's age, rolled in lilac, satin bed sheets. She looked up, at Stephen.

'Happy?' he said, and she nodded, thinking. What he'd meant when he said she went on about them all the time was that she occasionally called herself flat-chested. But she'd never considered this to be an insult or an attack. She'd always been content with the size of her personal assets. It was Stephen who found them disappointing, although she hadn't realised this until three years after their wedding.

It was at a party for the retiring cleaner at the insurance company where David was MD and Victoria was office manager. David, one of the sales ledger clerks, had brought his girlfriend, a glamour model who worked freelance for the Sunday Sport. Stephen had always claimed David was too young and contemptuous to work for the company, but he flitted around David all afternoon, pouring his wine, patting his shoulder. 'That's a nice girl David's found for himself,' he said, while they opened bottles together beside the facsimile machine.

'Nice cleavage you mean?'

'Well, I'd be hard pressed to find *your* cleavage, Vick,' Stephen replied, proving that was indeed what he'd meant.

David, who was eavesdropping from the canteen doorway, winked emphatically at Victoria.

'New Year, new body!' said the porter as he wheeled Victoria down the corridors of the clinic on the third of January the following year. 'Don't think of it as an operation, it's just an upgrade.'

Victoria had accepted Stephen's offer because, now she was thirty, it seemed like an easy way to push her 'best before' date further into the distance.

'If you have no opinion on your chest,' her sister had said, 'it shouldn't matter either way. Me, I'd jump hoops to get some implants. You're looking a gift horse in the mouth, you are.'

Anaesthetic killed some people and Victoria couldn't help thinking that she was going to die for the sake of vanity, like the girl from the movie *Seven* who had a choice to live with a disfigured face or die by wine and paracetamol. She'd be a statistic in a magazine article to discourage teenage girls from messing around with their God-given. She might never even get to buy the DD bra.

In the theatre she'd stared at the clock on the wall, her hands wrapped around her chest like wings, still hesitant. 'Okay, start counting,' the anaesthetist said, 'by the time you get to ten you'll be asleep.' He did say asleep, but Victoria heard, '*gone.*'

She woke up groggy, three hours later. Her chest was bound like a nun's in cream bandages. Her thick hair was stuck to her head with sweat. There was no mirror in her private room. She'd seen this before on television – they wouldn't let patients look at themselves until they were healed; their noses would be bruised from filing, or their hips scarred from liposuction. Now it was over, the thought of surgery didn't seem quite so grotesque. It was a bit like having your ears pierced – you only realised afterwards that it didn't kill you. She couldn't work out if the bursting pain under her bandages was her modification or her heart jumping with the joy of survival.

A week later, Victoria left the clinic. She undressed in front of the full-length mirror in the bedroom. Her surgeon had told her that her breasts were still swollen, that she wasn't to be alarmed by their size, and that they'd shrink gradually over the winter. They were big, but perfectly round, like cantaloupe melons blushing in a supermarket aisle. She lifted one and saw the pink slash-scar underneath. She let it drop again and turned sideways. It was the first time her chest had protruded further than her stomach, like a Barbie doll. She went to her underwear drawer and tried her string bikini. Her skin spilled out around the cups. The white triangles only covered her nipples, like models from South Beach in hip-hop videos, a butterfly without the butter.

When Stephen came to bed that night, Victoria was an elongated lump under the duvet. She kept her eyes shut and concentrated on breathing as if she were asleep.

'Well,' he said, addressing the darkness in general. 'Is there something you want to show me? I know you're not asleep.'

There was laughter in his voice, as though he was expecting to join in a game of hide and seek. Some kind of foreplay initiation.

'Vick?' he said.

Victoria sighed, wriggled out of the toasty cover, and flicked on the lamp on the bedside table. It was typical of Stephen to buy her a birthday present that was really for him. She squinted up at his face through the unfamiliar light. His features were bombastic with excitement, like a child at the front of a roller coaster queue. She gathered her old cotton T-shirt up to her neck and laid there, waiting for his reaction.

'Oh...' he said, and his speech trailed off as he realised there was no suitable adjective in his vocabulary. He undressed quickly and crawled onto the bed, sidling toward her, his eyes wide and expectant. He hadn't had sex with his wife for eighteen months, ever since he made that thoughtless comment at the office about her non-existent bust. He thought the operation was a glib gesture, an unspoken apology, a plaster-cast for her libido.

Victoria glared at him. 'They're sore,' she said, as he reached his hand up to her chest, his fingers pinched, ready to tweak a nipple. She curled away into her usual foetal position, turning the bedroom black again. She supposed there was nothing wrong with looking. The surgeon had seen them after all; but *David* would be the first to touch them.

Victoria had been sleeping with David for a year, every Wednesday in the boardroom after the weekly sales meeting. She used to worry about getting caught; she'd have to live without Stephen's salary. But she'd realised money meant nothing while she lay healing in the clinic. Stephen had bought her every goddamn material possession known to man and she still didn't fancy him.

David wanted to marry her, he said, but she didn't believe him because he dated twenty-five year old page three girls, blonde *and* buxom. Last year Victoria was only one of those things, but it was a new year now.

The following Wednesday at the sales meeting, Victoria wore a thin white blouse, open to the third button. David gazed over the table at Victoria's cleavage. So powerful was his stare it that caused her to look down and admire her body too. She'd never really understood why women wanted tits. Surely nobody wanted people to talk to their chest instead of their face, to bear unnecessary weight like an albatross. The penny dropped at the sales meeting. Men loved flesh, the sillier its shape, the better - they were easy creatures to please.

When the saleswomen left the room, Victoria and David stayed back to clean. She was leaning half-naked over the manager's chair when she noticed Stephen watching dumbfounded from the projector plinth. His mouth popped open and closed for a few seconds, like a fish testing its water for oxygen.

'But they're my tits,' he said finally.

'Right now, Stephen,' David said, his voice still husky with sex, 'I think you'll find they're mine.'

Victoria giggled like a schoolgirl, then she stifled it, her hand to her chin.

tell tales

Path

Mark Rowe

Y ou could say we've reached an understanding, them and me. They took Carol first, then my organs, then my joints, my health and my mobility. So I didn't have a choice, really. That's why I still have my brain.

They came from the sea. This house used to be an inn, perched close to the cliff top, one of those places they say will fall in one day. I don't care though – I'm old. It's a big place, five bedrooms, a large kitchen, a washroom, two bathrooms, and a dining room joined to a living room with a bar. It's all beautiful oak inside, pretty worn now. Since we closed the business it has gone to pieces. I welcome this deterioration. There's a path down from the house to the shingle beach with railings installed by the council. I'm sure that the house is closer to the edge than eleven years ago. I can see why people say it's going to fall in: it looks too tall for its width, not quite plush with the horizontal; the upper storey overhangs in an unstable looking way.

The sound from the sea below will keep me here at least until I die. Always the same elements, always different, changing every instant that you listen to it. Thirty plus years ago I used to help with the sound at rock 'n' roll gigs, and the scream of feedback and tinnitus has stayed with me. They go well with the sea, my damaged ears. What a crazy sound, scherrschwoosh, woosh, scherrschwoosh, woosh.

We were going to stop taking custom anyway as we'd saved enough, but that night cemented the decision. Carol and I felt uneasy going into that guest room afterwards. Eleven years ago. It was one of those nighttime winter storms that planted fears of toppling in us. The wind and rain played the house with roars, clatters and creaks, the ever-present sound of something out of sight straining to give. Our only guests, a young couple from Surrey, were at the bar, trying not to look terrified, which amused me. It was late, but they were too frightened to go to bed with the notion of waking in mid-air, on the way down to sea and rock. Carol kept their glasses full to send them to sleep: it wouldn't have done for us to leave them in the bar alone.

The noise was tremendous. I still wonder how we heard his knock. It had what one could call a special quality, its timbre separating it from the chaotic din. It certainly wasn't a loud knock, almost feeble, but still we heard it. I don't know why he didn't use the bell.

I opened the door carefully to prevent the wind from smashing it against the wall, Carol behind me, equally curious to see who was calling at that hour in that weather. The man at the door was a mess. I've never seen anyone that wet before, unnaturally wet. He had the remnants of a shirt on his torso, dark cotton trousers, torn, and one sock. His face, hands and chest had some small rough cuts, and there was a hint of blood in his brown beard. His voice was thick, but hoarse.

'No-one else left...All drowned except for me...'

He faltered at the threshold, then fell before our disbelieving eyes.

I could hear him delirious the whole night. The doctor came and said that he just needed sleep, no signs of hypothermia, no serious wounds, only fever. Carol said there was no point my hanging around; she was more than enough to tend to him, but with all his cries and talk I couldn't sleep anyway. Carol said it was like a conversation, but with his voice carrying the others. She found it unsettling.

'Such a good plan. It was a perfect day...rich, our families...Good to see you again...We still have it, we won't let them take it from us...for your lovely family, for your lovely Ruth...Where is it? Come back with us...claim your share...we need you, shipmate...'

And underneath his babbling, scherrschwoosh, woosh, scherrschwoosh, woosh. Louder than ever.

He died just before dawn, Carol dozing on the chair by his bed. She told me that she was sure she woke up immediately, knowing what had happened. She said she might have heard the rattle. The doctor was mystified, the coroner too – he just died. I saw him. His expression was the same as at the door, eyes wide and staring beyond, mouth very slightly opened.

I could see the vessel from my bedroom window, broken in two on the rocks a couple of hundred yards out from the beach. A shocking and sad sight. A mystery. It was a fishing boat but they weren't fishing. No-one could say what they were there for. Police in suits from the City came down. Some stayed with us. Polite blank faced men, they didn't reveal a thing. Three of our stranger's companions were found onboard. The rest must have been washed out to sea. No-one could even tell for sure how many were on board. No-one talking, at least. Then one day they took the wreck away. This didn't deter our visitors.

Clive and Eamon Humphries considered themselves the most successful scavengers that first morning when they picked out that chest. Fat lot of good it did them, though: they weren't right afterwards. They wouldn't say what they found in there, but Carol said that Eamon's Laura hinted darkly that whatever it was turned them. Something about seeing the reflection of their own skulls in the waterlogged chest, naked. Premonition of death and all that. They did die pretty sharpish too, Clive from the cancer, Eamon from the heart. Can't read too much into it though: the brothers never lived right.

I haven't been in that guest room since Carol passed on. It's not right for anyone to go in there, besides them. I saw on television a theory that stone can act as a recorder, replaying powerful events of the past, so perhaps it is an echo that I hear from that room every night. Those same words, over again, every night. Or they might be revisiting an old interrogation, trying to prise more information from the situation.

They have always been prompt. Six of them, a stout man, a tall thin man, an old man, a stooped man in a yellow mackintosh, face forever hidden; a scar-faced man, and the captain, with his dark blue, thick woollen jumper, his blonde fortnight's beard, and his cap. At first I thought that the drenched man would come with them, but he never has. Perhaps they leave him at home, where they're from; perhaps it's a punishment.

They come most twilights, following the same

pattern, but with permutations. The first time was three weeks after the stranger. There was a violent pounding on the door. I rushed to it, but it opened before I got there, and the six of them shuffled in, eyes burning but not looking at me. The door shut and they ignored my remonstrations and marched upstairs to outside the guest room where their friend had died. They stopped outside the door and the captain glared at me. Horrified, I lurched back into the living room. Upstairs a door opened, several pairs of feet moved, a door closed, and the voices started.

Three days later, I waited outside for them, ducking low by the car. I saw them come up the path from the beach as a gang. They seemed to be muttering, but I could not hear them. The captain led the path to the door: it is he who hammers with his left fist hard above the knocker. The next day I waited at the edge of the cliff, flat on my stomach, looking down, something I had never done before. Quite exhilarating. And I saw them emerge from the sea, heads first, as if they were merely walking up a hill, in rough double file, the captain at the fore, eyes glowing even at that distance, water dripping off them. They stopped briefly on the beach, waves at their feet, congregating for words I couldn't hear, then off up the path.

I watch them quite regularly now, not bothering to conceal myself. The basics are always the same, but there are variations. Sometimes they linger on the beach longer, kicking around rocks, pacing with their heads down, looking for whatever it is they are looking for. Sometimes the captain heads up immediately and they follow. Occasionally, the captain slaps the stout man on the back of his head, or shakes the thin man, or lowers himself to the ground, bending his knees. Whether he is looking or thinking, I do not know. They can appear quite amiable towards one another as they approach the house, but they can also appear sullen and withdrawn. The hammering on the door always sounds the same, though.

While we didn't accept them, things got worse. Carol never even acknowledged them, pretended I was being daft. The poor sweet thing knew though, I'm sure. It was just her way of dealing with them. Always the more grounded of the two of us. I knew they were real, but I didn't want them inside and I'm sure that's what made them angry. That's why Carol went, so slowly. That's why my organs started dying, that's why my bones hurt and my muscles have wasted away. I learned my lesson and my duties. I leave stuff for them now, like a bit of meat, some milk, some whiskey, sometimes some old clothes laid out on the bar. They never take any, but they don't seem unappreciative. They'll be men of principle. I keep the bar lamp on at night for them.

I never see them speak aloud. I only hear them when they are upstairs, and then it is the same combinations. But I'm sure they do speak between themselves. They just don't trust me enough yet.

I love my daughter as only a father can, but I am also starting to hate her. Took all the petty bits of her mother and little of the magic. She says I'm mad and keeps trying to take me away from here, but even she has stopped bothering me so much now. The council have given up too. Just waiting for me to snuff it, now. I hope they're holding their breath, the bloody bastards.

They come most nights now. Passing custom, I call them. I hope they share the joke. It's a very distinctive sound they make on approach, a little like the sound of a helicopter's rotors, 'Flup flup, flup flup', and some quiet squelching. They smell of the sea, of course. Iodine and the other stuff you find in that water.

I am no paragon, but I would say they don't look too good. Their skin is very pale with a blue tinge. They look drawn; even the stout man's cheeks are hollow. Criss-crosses of cuts and new bruises mark their faces, evidently caused by hard falls on rock, metal and wood. The cuts are bloodless, washed clean by the sea.

When I go, I don't know if I'll join them. After all, as they themselves make clear, they are a special case. I like to think that I might. See, I think they have an underwater city down there. Maybe real, maybe just spirits, but some kind of city. Like London or Manhattan (which I will never see now). I like the idea of that. Skyscrapers and seaweed decorated bars, bright yellow taxis distorted behind undersea light. That'd be real pretty. It'd be a perfect place to retire, shooting billiards under there, Carol at the bar.

Near dusk I go to the cliff side and listen to the sea. I hear the same sounds, but different as always, and their question to him, 'So what's it going to be?'

Go, don't go, I don't know. Perhaps go, one day. I don't think I'll be in this world for much longer. What a crazy sound, scherrschwoosh, woosh, scherrschwoosh, woosh. It gets louder every day.

Music for Cold Weather

Lane Ashfeldt

Kaisa and Jaak had been together a long time.
Two years nearly.

When they left art school, Jaak got a proper job and stuck with it, while Kaisa zigzagged about all over the place being inspired. She'd try three different jobs one month and be unemployed the next. When they talked of finances, she said truthfully that money didn't matter to her; the last thing she wanted was a new-build log cabin in a forested suburb with all mod cons and nice neighbours. Their tiny flat over a launderette was fine by her – at least it was central. The last time he remembered Kaisa saying this was when she took on a position as junior stage manager at Turku's only fringe theatre, a job she adored right up to the day she quit, two months later.

It was after her stint at the theatre that Kaisa began organising parties for friends, which was how she got going as a DJ. Jaak liked listening to her play records, sure, but after a while he got bored by the parties and the half-heard small talk, and stopped going along. By this time Kaisa had built up a rep locally and was out past midnight three or four nights a week. He missed her like crazy. He'd wait up till she got home to hear all her stories, and the next day, before going to work, he'd make her breakfast in bed. When she started to get gigs in Stockholm and Helsinki he was convinced it was the end for them, but he tried hard not to show it.

The lease on the flat ran out so he went ahead and bought his log cabin, one of ten new-build homes in the forest thirty kilometres outside Turku. Buying the cabin was one thing Jaak could do that *he* wanted, and anyway, he had a feeling that before long Kaisa would be gone for good.

The day before his birthday, Jaak took the afternoon off to drive Kaisa to Turku's tiny airport. She was off to do a one-night spot at the Melkweg in Amsterdam, then on to London for another two nights. It was the most prestigious booking she'd had; in fact, she only got the call after some big shot East German DJ pulled out of the line-up.

The flat bleak fields that surrounded the airstrip were covered in fresh snow, and Jaak began to hope that the airport would be closed. But when they got there, he saw the snowploughs had been and gone, the runway's share of the latest snowfall carted off to the snow dump. Nothing, it seemed, would prevent Kaisa from leaving.

He found an empty space in the short stay car park. She looked at him as she lifted her bags from the car, her face pink with cold under her fur-trimmed hood.

'Sorry about the timing, Jaakko, but you know this isn't one I can turn down. Sure you won't come along?'

He shook his head and followed her into the departure hall. They stood at the Fragile Items counter watching Kaisa's aluminium record cases being weighed and stickered.

'I'll shout you the plane fare,' she offered.

Jaak shrugged, then smiled and ruffled her fringe. 'You can't afford it, baby.'

'I'm getting paid this time. You'd be surprised.'

He kissed her.

'Thanks for the offer. Maybe next time,' he said. He hated tagging along to her DJ events even more now they were full of cute people, which mainly meant cute guys. Why was that?

The next morning, when he reached into the cupboard for a jar of ground coffee, Jaak found a package wrapped in shiny red paper. The gift tag read, '*Hyvää Syntymmäpäivää* Jaakko. Sorry I can't be with you this time. Save my puzzle for tonight or you'll be late. xx, K.'

While the coffeepot procrastinated, Jaak stared out of the log cabin window. The view was rural but unexciting: the same flat white snow as yesterday and last week, the same unrelenting snow that would cover Finland for another two months. He tried to think of something useful to do in the four minutes the coffee would take to bubble through. He couldn't wash up because they were out of washing-up liquid. If he was quick, he could load the laundry into the machine, but he'd probably get distracted and burn the coffee and then be in a bad mood until lunchtime. In fact, he couldn't think of a single thing to do but rip the red paper from his present.

A cashbox. Kind of amusing, since Kaisa so rarely had any spare cash. She had her lifestyle to maintain, all that obscure vinyl to collect. As far as Jaak could tell, even the local weddings and private parties where she'd learned to DJ had paid better than the art house gigs she did these days. So why a cashbox? Jaak turned the key, opened the lid, and looked inside.

Scratched brown painted metal. A smell of dirty notes. Maybe a promoter had given it to her one night when the door take was so low there'd been nothing else to pay her with.

The coffee pot began to bubble and he swiped it from the ring, reduced the heat, and poured milk in a tiny pan to warm before turning his attention to the box again. With a deft movement, he lifted out the empty coin tray. Underneath it was a home-pressed CD that he slotted straight into the drive of his laptop.

Kaisa was right; he *would* be late for work if he hung about here listening to music. Never mind. He'd take in the blueberry pie Muumi had made for his birthday; his co-workers would cheerfully scoff the pie and overlook his poor timekeeping.

Cranking up the volume, he heard a vaguely familiar lo-fi intro. He knew her style so well: the textured ambientscapes that veered into vestigial memories of dub or drum'n'bass, sprinkled with obscure rhythms and textures that he wouldn't get until she told him where she'd lifted them from.

The sound quality was excellent, the best he'd heard on one of her recordings. But what was it about? On the gift tag, she had called it a puzzle. If there was a coded message it had to be in the lyrics. Eked out over maybe twenty minutes of track, the words were cut up, dropped in, scratched up, scuffed.

Midnight train, ramblin', [car horn]
All night long I'm [car horn, car horn]
Been losin' all my [bli-ip] and it really is funny, umm
badda dum.

A penny for a spool of thread
A penny for a needle
[Bli-ip] can't buy it...baby

The way she had used sounds to mask the occasional word; was that part of the puzzle or just a way around the legalities of sampling, that three second limit she had told him about? Jaak felt the urge to get wasted – that way lay clarity of musical perception — but Muumi's blueberry pie wouldn't stretch to him going into work late *and* off his face. He poured the dark coffee and watched it lighten when he added warm milk.

Some of the ambient sounds he could figure out: the bleep of a car's central locking system, the high pitched 'bli-ip' of a barcode scanner, a metallic shuffle that could be a home-made percussive or the muffled clink of a pocketful of coins. Wordless interludes were broken up every so often by snatches of sampled lyrics. The singers? Contemporary pap rap stretching back to Elvis and beyond.

I finally got my baby about half past three,
She said I'd like to know what you [bleep] with me.
You think you gotta keep me iced
You don't
You think I'm gonna [plink] your [clink]
I won't
Sex can't [bleep] it...baby

Jaak screwed up his face in concentration as he took the first sip of hot coffee. He had to admit that this was just as well produced as something by a real band. Maybe she hadn't dirtied the samples enough to get clearance for radio, but she'd get away with it in clubs. Then, if the big boys wanted to play ball with her, their lawyers would cut her a deal. The track was a kind of progress, proof Kaisa wasn't messing about this time.

All the same, it was unlike Kaisa, he thought, to make a song about money. What was her point? Did the rearranged lyrics hold a hint of complaint directed at him?

The Elvis song he knew. He sang it along in his head until he came to the chorus: 'Money, honey'. Some of the other songs were on that theme too, but he didn't know them all. That barcode blip she was using had to be code for money: *'been losing all my [bli-ip] and it really is funny'*. And *[Bli-ip] can't buy it...baby*.

Jaak gulped at his coffee, burning his tongue. For as long he'd known her Kaisa had been unconcerned about material things, but now she was changing fast. Without ever seeming to have mapped out a career path, the girl seemed to be gearing up to go global. If that happened, she'd get paid a serious whack to do what she loved. At some level Jaak felt easier dealing with the broke Kaisa he knew. If she ever became stupidly rich, or even moderately self-sufficient through a lump sum from a one-off hit single, then why on earth would she still need a boyfriend from suburban Turku?

My baby gives me the finance blues,
Tax me to the limit of my revenues.
Aha-ahaaa, all the things I could do.
[Bli-ip, bli-ip, bli-ip]
Must be funny
In a rich man's world
Drugs can't [bleep] it...baby

Jaak went to eject the disc from his laptop. That's when he saw the scrap of paper that had dropped from the plastic CD case on to the keyboard.

'THE PROBLEM WITH BIRTHDAYS IS YOU'RE MEANT TO ENJOY THEM, YET

NOBODY EVER BUYS YOU THE RIGHT PRESENT. THIS BIRTHDAY, I PROMISED YOU A PUZZLE. YOUR CHALLENGE IS TO SELECT YOUR IDEAL BIRTHDAY PRESENT FROM THE FOUR OPTIONS BELOW.

1) I'VE FOUND A RICH NEW BOYFRIEND. CHOOSE YOUR TOP 10 OF MY RECORDS TO KEEP AND I'LL SEND A REMOVAL FIRM FOR THE REST.

2) THERE'S A QUEUE OF GROUPIES LINED UP AT MY MIXING DESK EVERY NIGHT. NOW IS YOUR CHANCE TO DITCH ME GRACEFULLY. GO FOR IT.

3) AT LAST! I'VE BEEN OFFERED A RECORD DEAL. CELEBRATE WITH ME.

4) AT LAST! I'VE BEEN OFFERED A RECORD DEAL, BUT ONLY ON CONDITION I SLEEP WITH THE PRODUCER. I HOPE YOU UNDERSTAND.'

Some birthday present. The last verse of the track played itself out while Jaak stared at the square of black paper, at its silver felt-tipped block capitals, each letter 'i' sporting a metallic halo that graphologists held to betray egotism. Even as he rehearsed what to say or not to say to Kaisa, Jaak knew exactly which present he wanted. He just wasn't convinced it was the option Kaisa wanted him to choose. They'd barely seen each other these last few months. She had spent days at a time away, and when she did get home she was always exhausted. No wonder, if she had started seeing someone else. A sleazy record producer or a rich and beautiful teenage fan.

Jaak grabbed his coat, keys and wallet and exited the house, slamming the door behind him.

Outside, it was colder than it had been for days, and the car engine wouldn't turn over. Jaak's patience was in short supply, but after the engine failed three times he forced himself to count slowly to ten before turning the ignition key again. As he sat there in the fridge-like metal box, counting out each number viciously, *1-thousand-and-1, 2-thousand-and-2, 3-thousand-and-3,* it came to him: that pitch black afternoon a few weeks back when he'd caught Kaisa curled up in bed at an absurdly early hour, reading a comic borrowed from her kid sister and filling in one of those trashy relationship quizzes. That was when she had given him the clue. 'I like these quizzes,' she said, 'they're so easy.' 'What do you mean?' he asked, and she told him, 'Number three is always the answer to go for, anything else is just for teenagers with a death wish.'

Jaak laughed. Three was his choice as well. It was the only viable response. Elated, he felt sure the car would start instantly, but made himself count up all the way to *10-thousand-and-10* before putting his foot down and wrenching the key. The engine finally kicked in and the car crunched its way over the crusty snow on the driveway.

Jaak was nosing the car out on to the road when he remembered, and he hesitated a moment, foot on the clutch; but there was no contest really. The people from work would just have to do without. He was saving that blueberry pie for when Kaisa came home.

Hieroglyphics of the Dead

Kamila Shamsie

'Look outside. Tell me what you see.'

'Stars.'

'Hmmm....but what are they *really*?'

Yasmin slid off her grandfather's hospital bed, fumbled across the darkened room, and pressed her nose against the window. Outside, palm trees stood in silhouette, marble fountains spurted, and trees drooped with the weight of their fruit, drenching the air in a sweet-sour smell of early summer's mangoes. She craned her neck, saw the clearest night she had ever seen. Such a multitude of stars. She was not surprised, when she cast her eyes from left to right, to see that the sky, too, was drooping.

'What are they? What are the stars?' her grandfather asked again, his voice a whisper.

'Eyes. Eyes of angels. Watching us as we sleep.'

Yasmin heard her grandfather shake his head, no, against the pillow. 'The stars are the hieroglyphics of the spirit world. They're the means the dead use to communicate with the living.'

The door opened. Yasmin heard her mother exclaim in surprise: 'Why are the lights out?'

She pressed a switch. Yasmin hid her face in her hands, hid from the sudden light, hid from the sight of her grandfather half the size he used to be.

'Almost time to go,' her mother said. 'Can I have a few moments alone with your Nana.'

Yasmin did not want to see the look on her mother's face either. She put her arms around Nana's neck and pressed her cheek to his.

'Don't cry,' he said, when she straightened up. 'See, you've wet my cheek.' But his other cheek was wet too. 'I'll write,' he promised.

The next night Yasmin huddled in the garden as mourners flitted in and out of the house. She knew she should be inside with the women, seated on the white sheet in the drawing room, scooping up handfuls of kidney beans and letting them trickle through her fingers as she murmured a prayer over each one. But still she sat by the bougainvillea, craning her neck upwards, searching for some new formation in the stars.

Rapid shots of gunfire cut through the air. Yasmin stayed where she was, looking up.

'Yasmin! Come inside. I told you never to step outside while that maniac's firing.' Her father swung her up in his arms and carried her inside.

'He's not shooting at me,' she muttered into his shirt.

'I know. He's just reminding the world of his presence. But bullets don't just disappear into the clouds; they have to hit something.'

'I would just like to remind you that you voted for him,' Yasmin's uncle said.

'For him?' her father laughed. 'I can't remember the last time I voted for someone. I just vote against their opponents...now where are you going, Yaso?'

Yasmin pushed herself out of her father's arms and pressed her nose against the glass sliding-door which separated her from the night.

Yasmin barely slept that night – she forced herself to stay awake until the stars dimmed and then disappeared, and the next morning she woke up early to the sound of cars driving up as the first of the day's mourners arrived. And kept coming all morning, all afternoon, and then in to the evening when the burial took place and the women prayed over kidney beans while the men took the body to the graveyard.

Finally, just after sunset, she rested her head again her mother's shoulder – just for a moment, just for a moment – and when she opened her eyes she was lying in bed and it was dark outside.

Yasmin glanced at her clock. It was after ten. She jumped out of bed and ran downstairs. Her mother called out her name but Yasmin was already out the front door. She ran around to the back of the house and climbed the winding staircase to the roof. Her feet skimmed up the concrete staircase so fast so fast, as near flying as she had ever been, and if she stopped for a moment to think, how high should I lift my leg for each step? how far to the ground? then surely she would trip and fall, for she was moving at a rate of sheer impossibility. With a final bound she was on the roof, staring into the stars.

And, nothing.

'Please, Nana,' she pleaded. 'Something. I need something.'

Don't try so hard, a voice inside her whispered.

Yasmin extended her arms to either side of her and started going round in circles, slowly first, then faster faster until her whole world was the intoxicating night smell of Raat-ki-Rani from the neighbour's garden and stars spinning, shifting, rearranging themselves into...into...a hand!

Yasmin came to a stop. There, just above her, the stars were a hand, palm-downwards, bearing down, yes, moving closer, sweartoGod, fourteen stars detached themselves from the sky and Yasmin closed her eyes to receive their touch on her head.

His hand always fit so perfectly on her head even though she kept on growing and the size of his hand remained unchanged.

Behind closed eyelids she saw the hand coming down closer, closer, any second now it would...

Dhud-dhud-dhudhudhdhud. Yasmin's eyes sprung open. A star fell from the sky. *Bullets have to hit something.* Her neck snapped backwards. Where the second finger of the hand had been just seconds earlier, there was only silvery-shimmering cloudiness. The blood of a star.

Yasmin looked to her left, at the rooftop down the road. The Minister stood there, gun in hand, surrounded by his lackeys who whistled and cheered.

'You can't shoot a star and get away with it,' Yasmin said softly – it was a promise and a curse. 'You can't.'

Almost a week later, Yasmin's uncle ran into the house, waving the evening paper in the air. 'Have you heard? Have you seen? Today in the National Assembly an unknown assailant approached your maniac neighbour and - oh God! I shouldn't laugh - and bit off his finger. His trigger finger. The assailant got away, don't ask how; you would think in a place like that, security - but still. A reporter was present with a camera, took a picture when the stranger grabbed the minister's hand, but there must have been a glass door or something in his way. The flash reflected off the glass and obscured the attacker's face. See, here it is.'

Yasmin ran forward, peered under her uncle's arm at the picture. Yes, there it was: the Minister, fear across his face, his wrist in the grip of a powerful arm that was pulling the Minister's hand up towards...towards...

Yasmin yelped, jumped backwards, danced her uncle around the room.

Where the assailant's face should have been, a star shone forth.

still. A recorder was present with a camera, too—
perhaps when the attacker grabbed the minister's arm—
but there must have been a glass door or something in
its way. The flash reflected off the glass and obscured
the attacker's face. See, here."

Yasmin ran forward, seizing upon Bernardo's arm,
at the picture. Yes, there it was, the Minister, Gene
against his face. His wrist in the grip of a powerful arm
that was pulling—the minister's... hand run
towards the word...

Yasmin yelped in pain, lurched wildly back. Her eyes
around the room.

Where the assailant's face should have been, a slat
stone return...

Sucking on Tamarind

Saman Shad

'Bismillah-i-rahman-i-rahim.' She whispers the words to herself and continues reading the verse from the Quran she's read at least a million times before. Every day, five times a day, for the last forty odd years. Her yellow cotton *dupatta* reeks of strong *ithar*, a concentrate perfume that actually leaves a taste in the back of my throat. She takes a deep breath, gathers her *kurtha,* and prostrates herself to the all mighty, all merciful Himself. Bowing and rising up twice, acknowledging the angel who sits on her right shoulder, and then the one who sits on her left. All the time words of a sacred text fly like feathers from her mouth. Finally she cups her brown crinkled hands (workman's hands she calls them) under her chin and gathers all her wishes inside them, holding both hands close to make sure that not a single wish is able to drip away before it is released to Allah.

I know what she is wishing for. It's the reason she's praying in my room. It is why I feel cold, even though it's the height of summer. The wish is writ large in her eyes. I can see it when she gets up off the prayer mat and gives me a look, a look only a mother can give to her child, and sighs. The icy chips of guilt spike through my spine and I cringe. This reaction confirms everything and fills her with a resounding feeling of satisfaction. A deep fulfilling sensation that is so much more satisfying than praying itself. She now knows; it wasn't a wasted wish after all.

She reads a surah to herself and comes over and blows a soft breath of warm air on me, before quickly biting her lip. I know what she wants to say. What she's bursting to say. But she can't do it, and I'm not going to invite her to do so. Why should I make this any easier for her? Yes, so things have changed. I have changed. People change. Especially when they move to foreign countries with different morals. They get new ideas, corrupting ideas, ideas that corrode values and crack the base of their cultural and religious heritage. Ideas that change them from people you once knew, to strangers.

But my mother only smiles, and gives me that innocent look of hers. How can you be almost fifty and still appear innocent? It is this, along with a spark that quietly exists in the corner of her eyes, that I find very unsettling. Always have. She knows this, because every time she gives me that look it gets the same reaction. Somehow the full weight of gravity asserts itself into my eyeballs and causes them to drop like dead, guilty marbles towards the floor. This time is no different. Leaving me to stand there staring at the ground, acting like I have wronged her for some reason, but not really knowing why.

To some outsiders – the family-friends and relatives kind – her actions may look like that of a devoted, loving, religious mother. But to me each one of her moves is filled with passive-aggressive rage. That's right, Passive Aggressive. I've learnt a lot in my time away. Learnt big western words, ideologies, and grave insights into the state of the mother-daughter relationship. I've come to question myself, come to look at relationships, especially familial ones, with a bitter and enraged eye. And then, after all that, after poring over Psychology texts at university, enlisting the help of behavioural therapists, counsellors and psychoanalysts (all the quacks who consider themselves to be scientists, she would think), while using therapy groups as back up, I've finally come to realise that no, this isn't really me either. I love my mother, pure and simple, and I know – she means well.

OK, she prays in my room so she can pass on the holy virtue of prayer to me by proxy. She wishes that I hadn't joined the covenant of Satan himself. She reads surahs and blows on me to ensure that the Horned One keeps away. But perhaps, just maybe, I'm looking at this all wrong. Maybe she truly believes that I can get an easier entry into heaven if she helps me along the way. Perhaps those looks that I accuse of wanting to afflict guilt are just looks of maternal concern. Maybe those surahs are meant to keep me safe, to protect me when she isn't around. Perhaps all she wants is to get closer to her daughter, and she finds that prayer is the easiest way to do so. Perhaps...maybe...I don't know.

The easiest way of finding out her motives would be to ask her. Just confront her and ask, 'Ammy, do you really think I'm evil?' But my continued indoctrination into the Western mindset prevents me from discussing my true thoughts. Instead, while my mother is putting her ruby-red prayer mat away, I grab her wrist and press it. Not too hard, but strongly enough. She turns and looks at me, eyebrows coming together, raising themselves towards the sky, but her lips remain silent. We stand there, mother and daughter, wrist in hand, not speaking. And she knows. It's not too late for me yet.

*

Anyway, all those things I said about group therapy and psychoanalysts are only partly true. I mean, I didn't do it purely for self-help reasons. I actually had to do it for uni, for the purposes of my continued stay in the merry shores of Great Britain. Good ol' Blighty, they call it. Grand Britannia. Where many an Asian person like myself goes to continue their education in colonisation. I am part of the growing brown tidal-wave that has been building ever since Partition, and which many a bulldog-owning, flag-waving Brit may secretly believe is threatening to overwhelm his or her tiny island.

My mother likes to blame this country for everything that is wrong in the world. Which may, if I was to think in that way, imply everything that is wrong with me. She has only been here twice, but is happy to speak with a conviction of experience that paints everyone with the same brush. They all have such sour faces, she will say, like they've been sucking on tamarind all day. Tamarind isn't so common in the UK, I inform her, so for her purposes perhaps she would like to change the point of reference to limes instead. She sniffs at that, like I'm trying to show her up or something. And the food! Oh the food is just hideous, you wouldn't even feed it to the servants, yet they serve it in expensive restaurants. Not many people in Britain can afford servants, I tell her; instead they enlist the help of TV shows to clean, renovate, and fix-up their house. She finds that utterly hilarious and thinks I'm trying to pull her leg. No, really, I say. But she doesn't believe me.

Perhaps it's too late to change her mind about the country. I mean, after all, it was the Brits who robbed her of her heritage. We lost all our land and fled to Pakistan with nothing but the clothes on our backs, she has told me many times in the past. We boarded this enormous ferry and everybody slept out on the deck side by side in lines like cargo. Forget beds or benches or even toilets! We had a bucket to do us the entire journey, and it fell into my sister's eight-year-old hands to empty it overboard. And your grandmother didn't help matters. She was so sick, so very sick, because of the sea, we thought, but it was all your uncle's fault. My brother had to plant himself in her belly then, didn't he? Arre, Sayrah, I remember it all like it was yesterday.

Should I *feel* something when she tells me this tale? Should I feel anger, should I feel hate? Should I be hurt at the injustice of it all? If they didn't have to flee India, if my great-grandparents hadn't lost their land, perhaps things would have been different, perhaps we could have been rich, perhaps things would have been easier. But somehow I doubt that. Instead I feel nothing. Not complete ambivalence or anything, just nothing. Like I don't have the emotional energy to invest in all the wrongs that have occurred in the past, when so many injustices continue to occur in the present. And all I can think is, how can she remember it like it was yesterday when she was only two years old at the time? But of course I don't say anything, because repeated conversations can be powerful enough to invoke a memory you never thought you had.

Like the time I was three and I got my head stuck in the railing of our balcony in Pakistan while trying to reach for a mango. I don't know why I decided I needed to reach with my head. Perhaps I thought if I got my lips close to the plump ripe fruit, I could eat it before any of the other kids spotted it. But nonetheless, the incident has been repeated to me so many times it's now part of my consciousness. I can almost see myself, through the hazy blur of memory, with my oversized head stuck like a watermelon between two metal rails. It wasn't my fault I had a large head. It's just one of the many things I blame on genetics. Luckily, I grew into it, and through the benefit of time can kind of understand why the neighbourhood kids used to call me Moonface. Sometimes, if I concentrate hard, I can almost feel the thick greasy ghee dripping down my neck as they tried to lubricate my head before pulling at my helpless little body. Come to think of it, it wasn't a pleasant ordeal. Maybe the reason I don't really remember is because I tried to block the memory out.

I don't think my mother ever tries to block anything out. She wants to remember everything exactly as it happened. She wants to carry all the emotions that accompanied the incidents she experienced before, inside of her. Carry the burden of all the rage, the hurt, the discomfort, as well as the highs – the joys, and the happiness. Carry these bundles of emotion wherever she goes, so she'll never forget. So the present can't take away from what she has been through and where she has come from. I used to think it was such a waste of energy to do what she did. To hold on to that excess weight of useless emotions. But now I realise these packets of feelings she stores inside herself are a part of who she is. The emotions define her. She is the sum of all the feelings she has ever experienced in the past. And when I think of it like that, it doesn't seem like a waste at all.

Ammy, I want to tell her, I've spent a lot of time thinking about you. And the more I think I understand you, the more I realise how little I know you. As her daughter it is even harder for me to believe we can be so different. I like to think of her as a base jumper, diving off mountains with her heart open and no fear of repercussions. She never walks into anything half-hearted. Everything, even the meals she cooks, are prepared with a velocity of passion. Most of the time she appears excessive. But it's an endearing excessiveness, because deep down you know she ladles out these open-handed helpings of love and generosity without wanting anything in return. And as much as I'd like to believe there is an ulterior motive to her actions, I simply must acknowledge, most likely there isn't.

Toxins

Valerie Mason-John

O nce upon a time in an African village, there was man who lived in a timber hut with his newly wed wife. She cooked, washed and cleaned all day. He attended to their plot of land and the few animals they owned. Their hearts were full of joy. The wife would sing all day and the husband whistled all day as they went about their daily chores.

When the sun went down and the moon rose, the wife expected to eat her last meal of the day with her husband, but the husband expected his wife to visit her women friends while he went off and spent the evening with his men friends. They never discussed what they would do with their evenings once they began living together; it was just an unspoken expectation of each other.

Soon the wife's singing became curses under her breath, and the husband's whistling became the slamming of pots and pans. When evening came the husband quickly bathed and would leave the hut before his wife had time to ask him where he was going. The wife would put out two meals on the floor and eat them both before her husband returned.

The wife decided, in her head, that he must be seeing another woman, because it was rumoured that she was barren. The husband decided, in his head, that she must be going through the change of life rather early and started to spend more time out of the home. This convinced the wife that he had a secret lover, and her curses convinced the husband that he had indeed married a menopausal woman by mistake.

After one month of living together, communication had broken down and it was like a battleground in the home. One morning, the husband exploded at his wife when she asked: 'Will you eat dinner with me tonight?'

'Yes,' he screamed. 'And I will be bringing some friends home too,' and he marched out of the hut.

The wife was so surprised by her husband agreeing to come home for dinner that she immediately became suspicious. All sorts of things began to toss around in her head.

'How dare you bring a whore home,' she replied.

The husband had fled from the hut before he could hear his wife's reaction. The wife convinced herself that she had heard him say 'a friend', and that this was his polite way of introducing his new woman friend.

She panicked: what if she didn't like her? He had vowed on his wedding day that he would only take one wife: was he really like all the rest, and how dare he invite her home without her permission? She told herself that she could cope; some of her friends shared their husband with more than two women. She would put on a brave face.

As she prepared for her husband's return she put dirt in his food, and flooded the floor with buckets of water while cleaning. When she was down on her knees, trying her hardest to make the floor of their hut slippery, her husband walked in with his three friends.

'These will make us happy. While you've been nagging, I've been out earning us a living. Watch this!' he jeered.

A snake wrapped around his torso leapt onto the floor and coiled itself around an empty bucket. She screamed, and froze with fear. The husband, recognising her distress, coaxed the snake back on to his torso, but it was too late. Unable to say a word, his wife turned to the cooker and threw the dinner onto the floor.

She was frightened, but didn't realise it; she felt out of control. Instead of pausing, she worked herself into a blazing rage by throwing all their belongings around.

The husband, shocked by his wife's outburst, screamed:

'I'm sleeping in the bed with the snakes, and you can sleep at the foot of the bed. I've had enough of your menopausal behaviour.'

How dare he call her menopausal, she thought. The wife wanted revenge. That was the final straw.

She was so full of hate that she wished for the snakes to bite him so that he could feel her pain. She wished that the snakes would poison him. She told herself that his suffering would make her feel happy.

'Don't worry, the snakes can sleep with you every night for all I care. I'll make the earth my bed,' she chuckled. This will teach him a lesson, she said to herself.

But the husband forgot all about her. He ignored his wife so much that he didn't even notice when she was bitten by one of his snakes and died. She lay slumped outside their front door until some of the villagers carried her away. When he went into the village square to do his tricks, the locals would hiss and say, 'There passes the Sleeping One.'

He would smile, thinking they were talking about his three snakes. He could not see what they could see, or indeed hear what they called out to him. All he cared about was the money he would earn; the brick house he would be able to build, the livestock he could buy, the fame he was acquiring.

Upon leaving the village square his pockets were always full of gold, as he had become a spectacle, making the village very famous indeed. But soon nobody came to see him to do his tricks anymore. He became deluded and told himself that the villagers were plotting to steal his snakes.

Not satisfied with the wealth he already had acquired, he began to consider his options. His mind became envious, his heart jealous of other people's good fortune, his mind bitter and twisted until his heart and mind stirred his thoughts into such chaos that he became full of anger, fear and hatred. In a fit of rage he screamed aloud: 'I will kill and skin my three snakes and sell them for a handsome price to a travelling merchant before one of those rogues steals them. This will make me happy. I will never have to work again. I'll show the villagers who is Chief around here. I will knock down all the huts in my way and kill all the people living in them in order to build my brick house and live the life of a Lord.'

That night he fell into a deep slumber: he woke out of his sleep quite startled. Peering down into his face was one of his snakes. It began to speak with the voice of his dead wife:

'You never loved me. You never noticed me. I died on your doorstep and you trampled all over me. You never once listened to me. I am so angry with you. I will not rest until I get my revenge.'

The snake wrapped itself around her master's neck so tight that he began to choke and gasp for air. The second snake became so full of fear, that he told itself he could see his master trying to kill his sister who was still trying to choke him to death. He panicked and coiled himself around his master's arms. And with all his strength he fought to prevent his master from throttling his sister, and then called out for help to his brother.

The brother is nestled up against his master's feet and has been silently plotting his revenge. He has never been happy. He never wanted to live an urban life, and hated being part of a one-man circus. Since the day his master bought him and his two siblings, he had been preparing his attack. However, his sister and brother had stopped him every time he tried to bite his master, and so instead he bit the wife.

Upon hearing the cry from his youngest brother, he puts his plan into action. So fierce is the snake's jump that he head-butts his master's rectum, passing through the body, and causing grievous bodily harm to the heart. Not content with this damage, he fascinates his master's brain, causing the man to go insane.

The man never earned another penny again and the snakes were thrown out into the village and survived one month before being killed by the beggar children living in the lanes.

"...u never loved me. You never respect me. Listen
to me now Boanlea and you trampled all over me. You
never once listened to me. I am so angry with you. I
will not keep hearing your abuses."

The snake wrapped itself around the master's neck
so tight that it began to choke one and then another. The
second snake became so full of fear that it coiled itself.
He could see his mother loving, which his sister who was
still trying to pull him to death. He punished part three
himself around his master's arms. And with all his
strength he could not sent his master from the killing
bite. "Boy" and the other called out. "Let him in." he said.
The brother reached up against his master's feet
and too had been silently choking down what he had not
been ready to take as you used to live again in life, and
had no great part of that that happened in all the day the
master lost it. I am and I knew it killed. He had better
preparing his spirit. However his sister, and brother
had stopped him every time he tried to bring so much
and sometimes he did so to him.

Upon reaching the top from the surface, the back of the
man began to him achieved. Here as the water drip
limbed cascading his head as it began pressing through.
His body and resulted in a world bodily harm to the head.
No content with the master who let him bring so there a
slight agony the might the confused.

The man never denied another poison because he had
always been known to have his wits and survived
one marth before being killed by the biggest animals
having the limit.

tell tales

Biographies

LANE ASHFELDT

Lane Ashfeldt is another of those people with more than one passport and no straight answer to the 'where do you come from?' question, but one thing she will tell you: she is not, and never has been, American. Twice, she has been arrested on returning to the UK after long absences. Once as a suspected terrorist, once for nicking whiskey on the duty free. Lane Ashfeldt's short stories have appeared on several fiction websites, and she reviews for the London-based fiction website Pulp Net.

RAJEEV BALASUBRAMANYAM

Rajeev's first novel, *In Beautiful Disguises* (Bloomsbury 2000) was the winner of a Betty Trask Prize and was longlisted for the Guardian First Fiction Prize. His is working on his second novel, *The Dreamer*, based on a short-story which won an Ian St James Prize 2001. He was the recent winner of the Clarissa Luard Award and an Arts Council Writers' Award and has published short-stories in various anthologies including New Writing 12. He lives in Manchester.

TANYA CHAN-SAM

Tanya Chan-Sam is a mixed race South African writer living in South Yorkshire. She has published poetry and short stories in various anthologies, including *The Invisible Ghetto* (Cosaw Press 1993) and *A Woman Sits Down to Write* (Women's Writing Workshops 2003). She is currently working on a novel.

SHARMILA CHAUHAN

Sharmila Chauhan was born in London to East-African Indian parents. She is a pharmacologist but has been writing fiction for several years. Her work focuses on the experiences of British Asians, particularly those living in London. She is currently working on a novel.

MAGGIE GEE

Maggie Gee's tenth novel, *My Cleaner*, comes out in August 2005. Her eighth novel, *The White Family* (2002), was shortlisted for the 2002 Orange Prize and the International Impac Prize. Her ninth novel, *The Flood* (2004), predicted a catastrophic tidal wave in a city very like London. Her first collection of short stories, *The Blue*, will come out from Saqi in 2006. She reviews for the Sunday Times and the Independent and is the first female Chair of the Royal Society of Literature.

ROMESH GUNESEKERA

Romesh Gunesekera was born in Sri Lanka. His first novel, *Reef*, was shortlisted for the Booker Prize and his most recent, a novel set on an island in the near future, *Heaven's Edge*, was listed as a New York Times Notable Book in 2003. His other books are *The Sandglass* (BBC Asia Award), and an acclaimed collection of short stories, *Monkfish Moon*. His fiction has been translated into many languages. This year he is a judge for the Caine Prize for African Writing.
More at *www.romeshgunesekera.com*.

HEATHER IMANI

Heather Imani writes poetry and prose and creates stories for children. Her work has been published in three other anthologies including *Kin* (ed. Karen McCarthy, Serpent's Tail, 2003). A recent MA Screenwriting graduate (Leeds Metropolitan University), Heather also writes screenplays. Her 15-minute script, *Soraya*, won First Runner-Up Prize in the British Short Screenwriting Competition in 2003. As one of ten writers selected for Arista Development's 'Scribes' script development programme, Heather is currently writing her second feature-length film screenplay.

Manzu Islam

Manzu Islam was born in Bangladesh in 1953 and came to live in England in 1975. He worked in East London as a community racial harassment officer and as an adult education teacher before joining the university of Gloucestershire as a lecturer in Literary Studies in 1990. He has written four books: *The Mapmakers of Spitalfields* (Peepal Tree 1997), *Burrow* (Peepal Tree 2004), *The Ethics of Travel: from Marco Polo to Kafka* (1996), and *Minor Visions: Postcolonial Ethics and Literature* (forthcoming).

Valerie Mason-John

Valerie Mason-John worked as an international correspondent for the Voice Newspaper. She is author of two non-fiction books documenting the lives of African and Asian women in Britain, plus a collection of her plays, poetry and prose. Her debut novel, *Borrowed Body*, was published by Serpent's Tail in May 2005. At the end of this year, Windhorse Publications will publish her book on Anger: *Detox Your Heart*. She works as a trainer in anger management and lives in London.

Biram Mboob

Biram Mboob was born in The Gambia in 1979 and spent most of his young life in West, Central and East Africa. His writing style is strongly influenced by his favourite works of classic science fiction, but his stories are inspired by the unforgettable experiences he has had in all the corners of Africa. Biram is currently hard at work on his first novel.

Tariq Mehmood

Tariq is a writer-co-director of the award winning film INJUSTICE (www.injusticefilm.co.uk). His first novel, *Hand On The Sun*, was published by Penguin in 1983 and his second, *While There Is Light*, was published in November 2003 by Comma. He also writes in Pothowari, his mother tongue, and is a founder of the Pothowari-Pahari language movement. *Kidnap*, Tariq's first stage play, has been commissioned by Peshkar.

Courttia Newland

Courttia Newland is the author of the critically acclaimed novels *The Scholar*, *Society Within*, and *Snakeskin*. He has contributed to the anthologies *Disco 2000*, *New Writers 8*, *Afrobeat* and *The Time Out Book of London Short-Stories*. He is the Editor of an anthology of new black writing in Britain, *IC3*, and of *Tell Tales Vol 1*. Courttia lives in West London and is an RLF project fellow at Birbeck College. You can visit his website on: www.myvillage.co.uk/urbanfactor.

Emily Pedder

Emily Pedder is a writer based in London. Her short stories have appeared in several magazines, and in 2000 she co-founded *Matter*, an anthology of new writing. In 2003 she graduated from the MA Writing program at Sheffield Hallam University and shortly after won a place on a mentoring scheme for new writers, supported by the Royal Literary Fund. She currently teaches creative writing at City University and is completing her first novel.

LEONE ROSS

Leone Ross is the award-winning author of two novels, *All The Blood Is Red* (ARP 1996) and *Orange Laughter* (Picador 2001). Her short fiction has been anthologized in *Dark Matter, Time Out London Short Stories, The Best of Horror and Sci Fi*, and the *Brown Sugar* erotica series. She has taught creative writing at Cardiff University, Trinity College Dublin, the City Literary Institute and the Arvon Foundation. She is co-editor of Whispers In The Walls (Tindal Street Press, 2000) and works at Roehampton University.

MARK ROWE

Mark Rowe was born to Ian and Pervin Rowe in Lewisham in 1976. He is currently working in London as an accountant and plans to complete a novel on corporate mythology between now and 2007.

SAMAN SHAD

Saman has spent time living in Pakistan, the Middle East, Australia and London. She has created plays for Hampstead Theatre, BBC Radio, Kali theatre, and has written pieces for various London colleges and schools. Her award-nominated play, *Lingering Voices*, premiered to critical acclaim at the Edinburgh Festival 2004. Her short story, *Normal Life*, appeared in an Anthology of Young Australian writers on which her first novel was based. She is currently working on a new literary piece.

KAMILA SHAMSIE

Kamila Shamsie is the author of *In the City by the Sea* (1998), *Salt and Saffron* (2000), *Kartography* (2002) and *Broken Verses* (2005). She received the Prime Minister's Award for Literature (Pakistan) and has twice been shortlisted for the John Llewellyn Rhys Award (U.K.). She is chair of judges for the Orange Award for New Writers (2005) and has written for various publications including The Guardian, Index on Censorship, Prospect, New Statesman and TLS. She lives in Karachi and London.

NIKESH SHUKLA

Nikesh Shukla, also known as Yam Boy, is a spoken word poet and musician from South London. His celebration of Indian classicism and the fiery polemic of political hip-hop has had him dubbed the Asian Chuck D. He has appeared on Desi DNA, as part of Stratford Theatre's 10 Poet Jam and on BBC 1Xtra as well as various literary publications. He has recently completed his debut album, a collaboration with Goonda-Raj, and continues to document the lives of second generation British Asians. www.yamboy.net

CAROL SIDNEY

Carol Sidney was born in West London to first generation

St Lucian immigrants. At school she wanted to be a journalist, but trained as a camera operator for television. She now works as a project manager in the performing arts sector. *Empty* is intended to be part of a series of connected short stories. *Turf*, her first completed story in the series, can be found in *Turf: Short Stories By New Black Writers* [Black Inc, 2004].

RACHEL TREZISE

Rachel Trezise was born in the Rhondda Valley in South Wales in 1978. She studied English and Media Studies at Glamorgan and Limerick Universities. As a freelance journalist she works regularly for the Big Issue. Her debut novel, *In And Out of The Goldfish Bowl*, appeared on the Orange Futures List in 2001. Her collection of short stories will be published by Parthian Books later this year. She is currently working on her second novel, *Sixteen Shades of Crazy.*

GEMMA WEEKES

Gemma Weekes - also known as MisFit and Goldy Loxx – is a feisty, young writer who's been published in anthologies including *IC3* (Penguin) and received much critical acclaim for her work in *Kin* (Serpent's Tail). She's also a poet, singer/songwriter, guitarist, workshop leader and journalist. Right now, she's in the process of finishing her first novel, *Redbone*, her first EP (rock/soul/and hip-hop eclectica), and avoiding Hackney Council. What she gets asked a lot is what she doesn't do, to which she replies, 'Sleep!'